PLEASE NOTE:

The names in this book have been changed to protect the innocent.
And also Lady Marry.

Also by Michael Gerber

Downturn Abbey,

an unauthorized parody,
in which members of the upper-class
embarrass themselves in front of the lower ones,
and vice-versa, by

Mr. Michael Gerber, B.A., N.O.C.D.

Lavishly, if only semi-sensically, illustrated by
MR. JOHN R. HOLMES of New York, U.S. of A,
as well as many other artists and photographers
whose identities have been lost
in the mists of Time.
Blast!

This book is dedicated to
the editors, writers and cartoonists of *The Wipers Times*
and the other "trench papers" of every nationality,
who used prose humor and cartoons to
endure the unimaginable.

First Cuckoo Edition / November 2012
ISBN: 1-890470-10-4

Attn design geex: This book has been set in period-appropriate type—Bitstream's
BT Cheltenham, with chapter heads in Brosse Demonstrator from Australia's
wonderful Greater Albion Type Founders (www.greater-albion.com). Non-
original llustrations are from Edwardian era sources now in the public domain.

If you enjoy this book, stop by www.mikegerber.com
for more good stuff, including new books, updates
and special fan-only content.

CONTENTS.

ILLUSTRATIONS.

April 1912 • Price: One Ha'penny

THE URCHIN.

Incorporating "Child Poverty."

BILL: Why are you crying? Don't you like cheese?
WILL: I am lactose-intolerant.

Win a trip to the HOSPITAL! Details inside!

CHAPTER ONE.

The Heartbreak of Male Heir Loss.
(April 15, 1912-June 1912)

I well remember my first day at Downturn Abbey. It was the morning after "the big canoe went down." Not what I took much notice of that—no one related to me was on the *Titanic*. In fact, no one related to me was anywhere. Back in those days, parents were a luxury, like protein, and I had neither. That's why I showed up at the back door of Downturn, my one shoe shined, my hair combed, ready to begin a new life.

At eight, I was a bit of slacker, but a natural impulse to better myself and avoid the considerable inconvenience of starvation had impelled me to the classified section of *The Urchin* magazine. Under a quiz called "Fifty Forelock-Tugging Ways to Drive Your Betters WILD," I spied a small advert for a "tray-boy" at the crumbling, half-wild estate just up the road from Ripping Foundling Home.

"Do you dream of a better life?
Travel? Excitement? Adventure?
Good luck to you. In the meantime, we require a tray-boy.
Long hours, little pay. Must be alarmingly small for age.
Full set of fingers required; mutes preferred.
Apply to Mr. Cussin,
Downturn Abbey."

As my eyes played over the tiny print, my calorie-starved faculties sputtered out a glorious future. First I'd obtain a left shoe. Then I'd rise up through the ranks, eating exotic, nutritious things like carrots, and rubbing shoulders with the great personages of the era... And then, perhaps, one of those personages would see something in me, a spark, something that recalled themselves at my age, and my chance would come. A chance to make good; a chance to show the world what I, Percival P. Percival, was put on this good green Earth to do.

For those of you unfamiliar with the workings of a great house—and in the case of Downturn, I use the term loosely; just how loosely you're about to find out—a tray-boy is a young male of approximately waist-height who follows members of the household, wearing a metal sideboard supported by his shoulders and crown. He is, for want of a better term, a sort of mobile end-table, and as human furniture, occupies the absolute bottom of the pecking order. But all work

Pre-Downturn days at Ripping Foundling Home. That's me in the middle, with the pointed hat. From left: Clive, Nigel, Clive Two, Othello, me, Mal, Reg, I forget, Reg the Git.

is honorable—so *The Urchin* serials had told me—and I was determined to be the best tray-boy Downturn had ever had.

"You'll be back before nightfall," predicted the Home's Matron, as fat as all of us were thin. "Say hello to Colin for us, will yeh? If he's still breathin'."

This was not idle speculation. Colin, an older, bigger boy and Matron's favorite, had for some years been employed holding up Downturn's subsiding North Gallery. Fortunately, Tray-boy is not as physically demanding a position as Foundation-lad, and offers much contact with the family. But this can be a disadvantage, if one cannot show discretion. These articles are, I suppose, a response to that—a clearing of the mental mechanism after eight years spent observing the most incredible things in silence. To be all of thirteen, for example, and see Lady Marry dance *Le Sacre du Printemps* in the altogether—I don't mind telling you, I nearly burst a blood vessel. And stroke was not the only peril; I later found out that the boy I was replacing, a chap roughly equidistant between Colin and myself, had succumbed to ether fumes while helping the Earl of Cantswim anaesthetize some butterflies. But I didn't know that then. Lucky for me, I didn't know anything. When I rounded the path and saw the estate for the first time, I was sure that great things were ahead.

• • •

I was met at the back door by Mr. Cussin, Downturn's fearsome butler. "You must be the new tray-boy. Come in." Something about the bright Spring morning must have offended him, because Mr. Cussin then uttered a string of words so foul that I assumed only orphans knew them. At first, I was frightened by the oaths and imprecations that constantly issued *sotto voce* from the man as he navigated a world that did not come up to his standards. Later, I learned it was a habit over which he had no control, any more than Mrs. Snughes could prevent falling asleep, or Craisy, Downturn's dogsbody, could stop herself from setting fires.

"Not the drapes, Craisy!" Mr. Cussin barked. "The fireplaces!"

"Sorry, Mr. Cussin."

"Never mind that. This is Percy, our new tray-boy."

"Pleased to meet you," she said. "It'll be nice to finally have someone underneath me."

"You go, girl," a passing housemaid cracked. Craisy blushed crimson, and skittered away.

"Nice talk," a slick-haired footman said as he streaked by with a gleaming silver salver. "Farm-girls only have one thing on their minds."

"Except when it comes to you, Dhumbas," said another housemaid.

"Dhumbas, don't forget the bicarbonate of soda for the table." Mr. Cussin pounded his burning sternum. "Cook is in fine form this morning."

Another footman approached; in his wide Yorkshire palm were two small blue objects. "Mr. Cussin, her ladyship asked me to put out these salt-and-peppers instead of the silver ones. I think it's some American custom."

"Oh Lord." The butler regarded the pair of ceramic hats with unbridled distaste. "Who or what are the Chicago Cubs?"

The footman shrugged—then noticed me. "New tray-boy? Welcome to Downturn." We shook hands. "A word of advice: never try to carry one of Cook's soufflés on your own; the last fellow got crushed flat. Or was he the one that got burned up? No, he suffocated! Anyway, we go through tray-boys at a terrific rate."

Anything I might say seemed likely to reveal the terror newly blossoming in my bowels, so I just smiled.

"Oh, I'm only chaffing you...You hope." Smiling, Killem turned to Mr. Cussin. "Doesn't talk much, does he?"

"If only the same could be said for the rest of you..." The butler handed back the little hats. "Put them out, Killem, monstrous as they might be." The footman walked away briskly, and Mr. Cussin sighed to no one in particular. "*Yanks.*"

•   •   •

They fitted me for livery, and measured me for a coffin, in case it ever came to that, and within the hour, I was standing by Cola, Countess of Cantswim's bed, getting used to the weight of the tray. I think I dropped everything at least twice, but her ladyship was exceedingly kind. Except when it came to the St. Louis Cardinals, who or whatever they were. "Promise me you're not a fan of those horrible men, Percy."

"I promise, m'lady."

"Then we'll get along just fine."

The lady of the house liked to read the paper as she ate breakfast, and clip coupons. Lady Cantswim had been born rich, as the heiress to a Chicago soda pop fortune, and planned to stay that way. One of her bromides was "Never give anything away."

I learned them all, that first morning. M'lady had a mother's habit of instructing every child with whom she came into contact, and so my eight-year-old self triggered an endless stream of maxims. "Gin makes you mean," "Never freeze mayonnaise," *et cetera*. We were rounding out our first hour together when Lady Cantswim said absently, "Every great fortune is founded on a great crime, little Percy. That's why I call my husband 'Robber.'"

His lordship burst in as if conjured, brandishing two telegrams and giggling. Whatever the Earl's faults, he was uncommonly free with the servants (and not just the maids, either). He would sneeze, cough, even blink in front of us, just as if we were real people. Robber, Sixth Earl of Cantswim, truly had "the common touch."

"Cola, have you seen this morning's papers? I've just received the most hilarious telegrams. But you have to read them together to get the joke." His lordship handed over two squares of brown paper for his wife to read.

"DEAR BORING OLD BOB
TITANIC IS AWESOME STOP
GOT LAST BERTH STOP
WHAT COULD POSSIBLY GO WRONG QUESTIONMARK
YOU ARE SOOO PWNED
COUSIN JERK."

"Now read the next one," his lordship said, barely able to contain himself.

"RMS TITANIC SUNK STOP
GREAT LOSS OF LIFE."

"Jerk changed his passage to make me feel like a country cousin—then— then—" The laughter began again, coming in great gusts. "What a git! What a stupendous, colossal knob!"

Her ladyship was not joining in. Silently, she put down the marmalade. "And did 'the knob' have his son with him?"

His lordship nodded in the affirmative, wiping away tears.

"Now Marry cannot marry him."

The Earl's laughter shut off like a tap. "Hadn't thought of that."

It was quiet. I coughed; uncomfortable silences make me do that.

"Who's this, Typhoid Mary?"

"His name is Percy. He's our new tray-boy." Lady Cantswim sighed. "I suppose all that cold water was good for young Onan."

"Cola, that nickname is cruel and unfeeling. Two of my family are dead. Now is neither the time nor place to bring up a young boy's quirks."

"Honestly, Robber. It wasn't a quirk, it was a compulsion. His last visit, your mother caught him fondling some art…Did you at least take out life insurance on them, as I asked?"

"Certainly not!" the Earl said. "To profit on my heir's death, it's unspeakable—"

"No, it was to give Marry something to live on if he snuffed it, which is what happens every time you Cantswims get near water."

"Cola, I have scruples. "

"Then you can be the one to tell your eldest she's scru'ed."

• • •

Cool and immaculate, Lady Marry didn't so much walk as glide over the pea-gravel, as she and the Earl did a circuit of the grounds later that morning. I trailed after them, balancing a plate of sticks for the dog. The dog's name changed regularly, owing to his lordship's shaky grasp on reality, but he loved the animal dearly, so we pretended not to notice.

The canine gamboled friskily, jamming its wet snout into Lady Marry's unmentionables. "Careful, pup, I'm back on the market again…Papa, what's 'pwned' mean?"

"Some code, I expect. Those dot-dash chaps have a word for everything."

She spotted a piece of gravel slightly larger in circumference than all the others, and made a mental note to inform Mr. Cussin. "I understand black for mourning, but why must we all wear life-jackets?"

"Marry, two of our relations have drowned. We most certainly will wear life jackets."

"But we're in no danger."

"That's what *they* thought!"

. . .

I soon discovered that I wasn't the only new servant starting at Downturn that day. Standing next to Mr. Cussin was a twinkle-eyed pear-shaped gentleman who winced painfully with every step... and yet oozed pure, unadulterated sex.

"Mr. Baits, this is Percy, our new tray-boy. Feel free to mistreat him."

"I'd never," Mr. Baits said, and I felt something very strange in the general region of my woolens. But before I could pledge my undying love, they were onto the rest of the staff.

Craisy scampered through, dodging a rolling-pin. "Craisy, you've met. And that voice you hear bellowing recriminations is Mrs. Phatore, our cook."

"Phatore? Poor woman." Mr. Baits flashed his common decency like other men flash a fat roll of bills. "I expect she was teased a lot, in school."

"School, nothing," Dhumbas quipped. "We tease her now."

LADY MARRY
in her full-body quilted kapok
life preservation gown.

"'No reason you should. Phatore's a fine old Yorkshire name," Mr. Cussin said. "This is our first footman. First name Dhumbas, last name 'Borrow,' as in steal."

Eyes flashing, Dhumbas returned to his newspaper. I thought I heard him mumble something about "myocardial infarction."

Mr. Cussin paid no attention. "Dhumbas is thoroughly evil, God knows why we keep him. On the other hand, he's balanced by our second footman, Killem, who's pleasant and laudable..."

"...so you're expecting him to snuff it?" Mr. Baits asked.

"As tragically as possible," Killem answered with a smile.

"Good man," Mr. Baits said as they shook hands.

A woman in black lay with her head on the table, snoring gently. Then she said muzzily, "Oh, Earl, I don't think we should, not here, not while Lady Cantswim is just in the next room—"

"That's Mrs. Snughes, our housekeeper," Mr. Cussin whispered. "She talks in her sleep."

Dhumbas leaned down and slowly whispered in her ear, "Titty clamps."

"Steady on," Mr. Baits said. "You'll poison her dreams."

"Just trying to give her a bit of excitement, Mr. Baits."

A woman with a face like the business-end of a shillelagh walked in. "Who's the gimp?"

"May I introduce his lordship's new valet. Mr. Baits, this is her ladyship's maid, Miss O'Lyin. Or, as I like to call her, 'Miss Fetal Alcohol Poisoning of 1877.'"

"Every fetus's got a right to take a drink if they want to. It's the law."

"Downstairs I'm the law, Miss O'Lyin, you'd do well to remember that. This is Gwon, our housemaid who embodies a changing society—"

"Someone's got to do it," Gwon said good-naturedly.

"—and finally Wanna Snogg, your love interest."

The valet grinned. "I'd hoped there'd be one of those."

"Nice to meet you, Mr. Baits. I'm mousy-hot and ready for action."

"Don't get stuck on me, Wanna. I'm bad news."

"Whatever do you mean?" she asked, backing him towards a corner.

"I'm a mysterious man with a murky past—"

"Keep talking."

"—and a troubled soul. I take others' secrets to the grave, and constantly do noble things which get me into desperate trouble. Don't try to save me—"

"Rowr," Wanna had him against the wall now, and was fiddling with his tie.

"No!" Mr. Baits cried. "You must stay away! I'm a puzzle, a riddle you cannot solve, a deep dark mystery that will bring you only pain!"

The rest of the staff stood transfixed. After all, this was the kind of thing people paid half-a-crown for, down in Ripping.

"Anyone mind if I climb on top of this gentleman?"

Just as things were about to get good, there was a sharp knock on the door, and the Earl walked in. "Hope I'm not disturbing anything—"

"Awww!" the whole staff groaned.

Mrs. Snughes woke up. "Just resting my eyes!"

•   •   •

As the cook loaded my head up with afternoon tea, I overheard Killem reading from his lordship's paper.

"Says here the word 'MIRAGE' was painted on the iceberg."

Craisy was hauling in a fresh bucket of cooking suet; she paused. "Really?"

"Yeah, and there were two people standing on it, in black clothes, smoking cigarettes."

"Get a move on, girl!" Mrs. Phatore brayed. "No one related to you was on that boat!"

"That's my line," I mumbled to Mr. Baits. He smiled.

• • •

"Smooth move, McGonigall's Laxative Powder," Miss O'Lyin sneered.

"Don't know what you mean," Dhumbas replied. "Went down easy as you please, just like we planned."

"And yet here we are, still among the peons." She struck a match off my cheek; so far, ashtray duty was the worst part of being a tray-boy. "What odds did the old valet give you?"

"Four millions to one," Dhumbas said, exhaling. "How was I to know he'd welch on the bet?"

"Skulking off in the middle of the night with all our money, that's a clue. And us going all the way to the North Pole with a bloody ice pick and a bucket of paint."

Drawing made by crewmember of the Carpathia, April 1912.

"Travel's broadening." Dhumbas ground out his cigarette. "Never you mind. One of my plans will pay off."

"Or they could sack you."

"They'd never, Miss O'Lyin. You neither. We're too important to the plot."

• • •

As Mr. Cussin always said, "A tray-boy in a great house sees all, hears all, and says nothing." When I was not actively serving the family, I would be standing behind a drape with only my shoes showing, ready to do whatever was asked.

For a few days, no one upstairs could bring themselves to discuss the issue at hand; the sudden break in the family line was too shocking, too awful, and as you'll see, at Downturn not saying important things was a way of life. Finally the Earl could take no more, and broached the topic one evening at dinner.

"There is an important issue that has arisen, something I'm sure each of you is thinking about, something that affects us all."

"Dad, you are totally right," Lady Unsybil said, whipping out a clipboard. "For too long, a free Tibet has—"

Her ladyship rolled her eyes. "Unsybil, I told you: no petitions at the table."

"But China's being totally harsh—"

"I don't see what business it is of ours," Lady Violent said. "Surely such matters are best left to the Tibetians."

"Granny, just because they're foreign—"

"Where ever does she get all these causes?" Lady Marry asked wearily.

"One of the Skelton boys," Lady Edict offered. "The one with the weird name who doesn't wash."

"Gramsci Bakunin Skelton is not a weird name!"

"Ow!" Lady Edict flushed. "Don't kick me under the table, bint!"

"Girls! No one is a bint!" her ladyship declared. "We can discuss the eccentricities of the Skeltons another time."

As his children squabbled and his wife refereed, the Earl felt his authority slipping away—almost as if it were happening not merely to him, at this table this one time, but to all people of his class, throughout society as a whole, and forever. Yet he persevered. "The issue before us is: What are we to do about Marry?"

"Marriage is all she is good for," Lady Edict said. "She's practically labelled."

"Yes, as if you were named 'Virginia.'"

Lady Unsybil snickered quietly, "*Awesome.*"

The Dowager Countess shifted in her seat. "I would be much less concerned, if Marry had a sweeter disposition. How does she expect to be married if she's so indefatigably stroppy?"

"Get knotted, Granny."

"See what I mean?"

"*Your* mother managed somehow," Lady Cantswim said. "Robber, explain again why Marry can't inherit?"

"It all comes down to primogeniture. From the Italian, I believe…"

"You see, Unsybil?" cried Lady Violent. "See what caring about foreigners gets you?"

"They're in the world, Granny."

"Only by divine oversight. Which the Empire is slowly correcting."

His lordship plowed on through the crosstalk. "…*Primo*, meaning first or best, and *genital*, meaning—"

Lady Edict's pale face brightened with sudden understanding. "So the first baby with the right set of bits, hits the jackpot."

"Roughly, yes."

Lady Marry pushed back from the table defensively. "Nobody's fiddling with my bits, I can promise you that!"

Lady Edict smirked. "Oh Marry, everyone's fiddled with your bits."

His lordship frowned; his wife and daughters seemed to speak their own private language, like the dot-dash chaps. "What do you mean, Edict, everyone's fiddled with Marry? Cola, what does she mean?"

"Nothing, dear. Just sibling rivalry."

"Tell that to Papa's old valet," Lady Edict snorted.

Lady Violent felt the conversation veering towards the modern, so she placed her fingers in her ears and hummed.

"I always wondered why he left in the middle of the night," Lady Unsybil said.

"Naked," Lady Edict added gleefully. "*Sobbing*."

Lady Cantswin and Lady Marry looked over at Mr. Cussin frantically. Hint received the butler rumbled, "I believe it's time for pudding."

•   •   •

By the end of that week, I had settled into the rhythms of daily life at Downturn Abbey. I was still undiscovered, and no great personages had stopped by, unless you wished to include two ladies hawking subscriptions to *Lo! The Journal of What Will Be*. But it was a pleasant place, where one could tell whom to befriend or avoid by how much they smoked. I was strangely drawn to Mr. Baits—as everyone was, even the Earl's dog—but I never felt I knew him. He kept himself to himself, which I suppose was a great part of his charm. There was a lot of exposition in that household.

I never could tell what was wrong with the valet, why he winced with every step, why there was a slight clanking in the vicinity of his gentleman's spigot. As a lowly tray-boy, I never had the courage to ask. However, I was passing through the corridor outside the servants' hall when someone else did.

"Well, well," said Dhumbas. "If it isn't old Master Baits."

"It's not the low humor I mind," Mr. Baits said, "it's the historical anachronism."

"Then you're in for a long book." The evil first footman crowded the heartthrob. "If you'd ever like to have a go, I'd be happy to accommodate you."

"Somehow I don't think you're talking about fighting."

"That's just the thing—you won't know until it's too late. Some dark night, I'll come from behind—"

"There are children present, Dhumbas. I'm warning you."

"You don't look so tough to me."

"Appearances can be deceiving. You know the Boer War? I did that."

"Aren't you the hard man? Let's see if you're all talk." Dhumbas reached down—then pulled his hand away as quick as if he'd been burned. "'Struth! What're you wearing down there? Armor?"

"As I've said, there are children present. Come along, Percy." And with the mystery no closer to being solved, Mr. Baits took my hand and we walked out.

●   ●   ●

It took only a telegram to the International Lavender Conspiracy for the Duke of Crowbar to learn of Lady Marry's changed circumstances, and one day soon at luncheon, Lady Cantswim announced brightly that the Duke was coming for a visit.

His lordship, however, was not so cheered. "I wouldn't get your hopes up, Marry."

"Why not?" Lady Cantswim asked. "With a new dress, a Wondercorset—"

"Crowbar's a nickname," her husband interrupted. "From boarding school. Let's leave it at that."

"Where did he attend?" Lady Violent asked.

"Beton."

"Oh, I see. That explains everything." When her American daughter-in-law still did not comprehend, the Dowager Countess spelled it out. "Do you know how they separate the men from the boys at Beton? With a crowbar."

Lady Marry and Lady Edict sniggered loudly; their sister didn't. "Can I just say? This society is totally heteronormative."

"Oh, you English and your old school rivalries," Lady Cantswim said lightly. She patted Lady Marry's hand. "Our daughter's more than a match for a little fabulousness, aren't you, Marry?"

•   •   •

Of course Lady Marry wasn't a match for the Duke's fabulousness; no woman was. After a dreadful evening spent discussing whether all the statuary in Downturn "mightn't look frightfully better with all those awful breasts and hips fixed," Lady Marry went upstairs to lick her wounds and curse her wrong bits. I, on the other hand, was dispatched to the Duke's room, for any nocturnal tray needs.

When I got to the Duke's door, I heard the sounds of a heated discussion, so I stayed outside.

"Who would believe you, a lowly footman?" His Grace was saying. "A Duke, DJ'ing at a club in Manchester? The very idea is preposterous."

"But I have *proof!*" I recognized this voice as Dhumbas's. Discretion told me to walk on, but my affection for Mr. Baits was stronger. I squatted down at the keyhole to have a better look.

"Proof? Are you speaking of these?" The Duke brandished a handful of club flyers.

"Give 'em over!" As Dhumbas lunged, His Grace tossed the incriminating cardstock into the fire. The Duke held Dhumbas back, as the glossy paper burned and the flames flashed colors. "Sorry, chum. 'DJ Crowbar' must remain our little secret."

Dhumbas shook himself free. "I'll get you for this," he seethed. "I want my 12-inches back!"

"You overestimate yourself." His Grace smiled cruelly. "Oh—you meant your LPs. I'll see if I can find them…Anyway, we'll always have Eighties Night."

Wearing a look of pure murder, Dhumbas thundered towards the door. I turned and scurried down the corridor just in time.

•   •   •

The entire household, upstairs and down, was dismayed over the Duke's hasty departure. "He even insulted my salt-and-pepper shakers," Lady Cantswim said.

"I don't think we can put it off any longer," the Earl said. "I am going to write my second cousin, Dratyew Crawly."

"So you won't fight for your daughter?"

"My dear, if this were a legal procedural I'd consider it, but as ITV ordered a costume drama, I think you had better reconcile yourself."

"Promise me one thing—" Lady Cantswim caught the Earl's arm as he headed for the library. "Make him *swear* he's not into dudes."

A CLUB FLYER
I found under the Duke's bed.

CHAPTER TWO.
The Twenty-Stone Nightingale.
(September-October 1912)

Long before he and his mother came to Downturn, I knew the name "Dratyew Crawly." Everyone did; he was the North's preeminent omnibus-chaser, and his bally great advertisements were everywhere. One couldn't go five steps without Dratyew's fair-haired, dimly handsome noggin grinning toothily at you.

"ET PIE WITH A ROCK IN'T?
GOT BOILS OR SUMMAT?
LOST A FINGER DOWN AT MILL?

Contact Dratyew Crawly, Esq.
The North's Finest Personal Injury Lawyer
He will fight for you!"

And now, "The Workingman's Friend" was here at Downturn, dining with the family. He did not make a good first impression—though, armed with the right bits in the right order, he didn't have to.

"Bit of an odd name, Dratyew," Killem wondered aloud.

"I overheard him explaining it to Lady Marry," Wanna said. "Mr. Crawly said his mother kept screaming 'DRAT YOU!' during labor, and it stuck."

"I'm sure she yelled a lot worse, but this is a family book," Miss O'Lyin said. "Even Dhumbas disapproves, don't you, Dhumbas? Wrinkling your nose like you just smelled a gaslamp—"

"Quiet!" Mr. Cussin commanded. "Dhumbas, Killem, help me carry up Mrs. P's trifle. And lift with your knees, I don't want to lose you to Dr. Clarkson like last time."

Mrs. Phatore's trifle was anything but—it was a lethal dessert, dreaded by all and only served to extremely unfavored guests. Nobody knew exactly how the cook made it so heavy, they only knew enough to keep it far from their mouths.

When the sweating, straining footmen appeared with the near-buckling tray, Dratyew was pointing at a large canvas over the Earl's head. "How much is that worth? Think I could sell it down in the village? How about that candelabra? Or this spoon?"

His mother Isapill Crawly slapped the utensil out of his hand. "You must forgive my son," she explained. "He is constitutionally unsuited for good news."

His lordship was gracious. "Understandable, given your line of work."

Lady Cantswim, too, was trying her best. "Is it true that after the *Titanic* went down, you had people walking the streets of Belfast in sandwich boards?"

Lady Marry leapt in. "You must forgive my mother. As an American on British television, she is forthright but socially unsophisticated. Tell me: does your penis prefer males or females?"

Lady Edict leapt in. "You must forgive my sister. There's something wrong with her brain."

Mrs. Crawly began rummaging in her purse. "Perhaps with the right medication..."

Lady Violent felt the dynasty teetering. "Mr. Crawly, we were speaking of the *Titanic*."

"Luckiest day of my life," said Dratyew. "80% of Third Class perished, but I made sure it took 80% of White Star with it."

"Mr. Crawly," Dhumbas whispered, straining under a small plate of trifle, "I wonder if I might show you an injury I sustained recently."

"Where?"

"It's...of a private nature," Dhumbas said, prospecting.

"No, I meant, where did it occur?"

"Right here, and now. This dessert is herniating me—"

Mr. Crawly disengaged immediately. "Oh, no. Anything that happens here, I would be liable for, and as the heir—well, I cannot very well sue myself..."

Lady Marry leapt in. "Mr. Crawly, I wonder if you know the ancient Greek myth of Andromeda and the Annoying Second Cousin?"

"You must forgive me, I don't. But the second part seems staggeringly familiar."

• • •

After dinner, Dhumbas poisoned the air downstairs by railing against the new arrivals. "Some friend to the workingman he is. Wouldn't even take my case!"

"I don't know, I rather liked him," Mr. Baits said. "Not every man would follow Lady Marry's myth with the one about Messalina and the prostitute."

Killem smiled. "Least we know how he swings."

"That's as may be, but Lady Violent looked ready to murder," said Mrs. Snughes, fourteen cups of tea keeping her awake for the moment. "First the dirty story, and then Mrs. Crawly asking to help out at the hospital—what's next? Anarchy?"

"Not if I can help it," said Mr. Cussin. "Tray-boy, come help collect the silver."

Every evening, the butler would melt down every utensil and refashion it, so that it was as new. Some people wondered why he took the trouble; but they didn't understand how Mr. Cussin felt about Downturn. They might as well ask why the butler clipped the lawn with cuticle scissors, or stayed up half the night blowing cool air onto Lady Marry's forehead. It was just how things were *done*.

Hours later, I was brushing the slag off my jacket and heading up to the hall for bed (I slept on a small cot, underneath the hall boy's bigger cot), when the housemaid, Wanna, stuck her head in the staff dining area. "Mr. Baits, might I have a word? Out in the corridor?"

"Certainly," I heard the valet say.

I watched from the shadows at the top of the stair, as Wanna slung a meaty leg into Mr. Baits' arm. "Wanna—" he said.

"YES!" she said.

"No, Wanna—really—"

"Yes, really! Right here! Right now!"

"I…cannot." Mr. Baits walked up the stairs towards me. He passed so close we nearly collided.

"Sorry," I stammered. The valet receded silently, clumsily, faintly creaking.

Wanna watched him go with a sigh. "Guess it's another night with Dr. Osbert's Oscillating Pommel."

· · ·

The Crawlys became a fixture at Downturn Abbey. His lordship took his cousin on long tours of the estate, showing him every crumbling façade, every choked and brackish seepage, every squalid cottage filled with ungrateful tenants. Decay and disrepair ran rampant throughout; Downturn's farmers had no idea how to farm, the gamekeeper allowed poachers to roam freely. Even I, who knew nothing of the running of a great house, could see that the Earl was in entirely over his head.

Like all people so cornered, his lordship buttressed his incompetency with a philosophy. "You see, Cousin Dratyew, the lower classes know how to do such things *instinctually*. Of course I could try to learn myself, from books and such— but that would destroy the natural order."

"Hmm…" Mr. Crawly seemed far away. "When you die," he mused, "do I inherit your corpse? Can one melt those down, for tallow or something?"

The Earl audibly swiveled in his tweed, locking eyes with his heir. "Each of us has a role to play, Dratyew. Theirs is to farm as best as they are able, get wet frequently, and perhaps starve. Mine is to look grand, and pack in as many big meals as I can. Who's to say which burden is heavier?"

Mr. Crawly opened his mouth, then thought better of it. His lordship clapped him on the back. "Don't worry, my lad, I can take it. We Cantswims are made of iron. That is why we sink."

They walked on, m'lord occasionally placing a small pebble on my tray. This was "fairy droppings," of which the Earl was England's foremost collector.[1]

The Earl sent this drawing, and many others like it, to the Royal Society. They did not respond.

I could never tell the difference between these exquisite specimens and regular pebbles, but I was a mere tray-boy. Ignorance was *my* place in the natural order.

"Cousin Robber," Mr. Crawly said, as they watched a sturdy yeoman hack at the ground ineffectually, "how does a person of your...remarkable nature keep from losing Downturn?"

"With great difficulty," the Earl admitted. "Things are always growing worse at Downturn Abbey; hence the name. My father, who was not nearly as intellectually gifted as I—by Jove, that's a whole fairy Stonehenge!—felt sure we'd have to sell the whole bally lot in the 1880s. But then I met Cola."

The farmer was plucking ripe carrots from the ground, cutting off the leaves, and then throwing the rest away.

"Might we tell him the orange part's for eating?"The Earl's look was answer enough. So Mr. Crawly searched for a new topic of conversation. "Cola's a bit of an odd name."

"Her father invented a soft drink. Staggeringly popular."

---

[1] Belief in fairies is not so uncommon in people of his lordship's generation, but the Earl came to it in a way that is, to my mind, worth conveying. The story I was told by Mrs. Snughes—who apparently heard it from the butler they had before Cussin—was this: The Earl's father had a secret shelf high up in his library, where he kept all the naughty materials—illustrations by Hogarth and Cruikshank, Sir Richard Burton's *Kama Sutra*, etc. One afternoon when the present Earl was about 12, he obtained a ladder and began educating himself with a will. Unfortunately a footman walked in unexpectedly, and the Earl was so startled that he fell to the floor. When he came to, his lordship apparently saw fairies; and so has believed in them passionately, from that day to this.

"So it's delicious?"

"Quite the opposite. But it contains both cocaine and opium. Drink one bottle and you'll go to the bloody ends of the earth for the next one."

The Earl swept his arm across the entire vista—the rolling green hills, crookedly plowed fields, and lightly smoking woods (Craisy must be about)—all of it crowned by the alarmingly tilted, but still quite impressive great house above them. "The world sees the great Downturn, stately, impressive. I see crates and crates of that dreadful 'Speedball Cola.'"

"I say, Cousin Robber, it's really tipping, isn't it?"

"Yes, remind me to hire more orphans."

"That can't be smoke, can it?"

A mini-megalith fell from his lordship's hand onto my foot. "Oh, my God! Quick, Tray-boy! We must save Downturn!"

•   •   •

The Earl and I hurried back to the house as fast as our legs could carry us. I found that if the wind hit me at the proper angle, my tray enabled me to actually achieve lift-off, and this allowed me to keep up. Mr. Crawly, however, made a regretful departure; a roller-coaster down in the village had killed some people, and Justice was whispering his name. We found an equally ugly scene unfolding in the library, where Mr. Baits, Wanna, and Lady Unsybil were loitering ineffectually.

"What's going on? What's on fire?"

"Only Craisy, m'lord," Mr. Baits said. "I told her to signal you, Indian-style."

"Blast! I was looking forward to being cool in a crisis! What is the point of being upper-class if one cannot display the special, very rare and precious characteristics that we, through centuries of education and breeding, have—"

"Well, there is a small crisis, m'lord."

"You mean this loudly dressed miscreant? Who is he, and why is he putting his feet up on my globe?"

"Nigel Foreshadowin'," the man said. He put down his magazine, and offered a card. The Earl glanced at it and dropped it on my tray. "I have a story to tell about your butler."

"We all have a story about Cussin. After a time you stop hearing it."

"Papa, tell how I was nearly christened 'goddamned C of E isn't bloody what it used to be, I can tell you that!'"

"Another time, Unsybil."

"Lord Cantswim," Foreshadowing said, "you've been housin' a sexual deviant."

"We've heard your story," Mr. Baits interrupted, "and the whole thing is preposterous. Just because a man wears a bra, that doesn't make him a transvestite."

"He could be using it for support," Wanna chimed in.

"Or to subvert conventional ideas of gender, revealing them as primarily social constructs," said Lady Unsybil.

"That's as may be, Miss, but take a look here." The bristly little man fished a crumpled and sweaty playbill out of his pocket, and handed it to his lordship. "Halfway down the bill: 'Morris and Doris.' I was Morris."

Red-faced and out of breath, Downturn's butler lumbered in like an armoire falling down a flight of stairs. "M'lord," he said, then looked daggers at the visitor. "I told you never to call on me here!"

"And Mr. Cussin was Doris," Foreshadowing said. "What did they call you?"

"The Twenty-Stone Nightingale o' the North. And don't gob on the carpet!"

"I did it because I know you'll have to clean it up."

Lady Unsybil saw the butler's agony. "Papa, whatever Cussin may or may not have done, this man here is enforcing rigid gender roles, and I for one don't appreciate it."

"Thank you, Lady Unsybil, but there's no need for you to defend me. What I did was indefensible."

"Oh, our act wasn't all that bad, Cussin old bean. Until you started swearing."

"You set me off, you devious rascal! You and your thievery."

Dhumbas appeared. "Did someone ask for me?"

"Unnecessary, Dhumbas, thank you." The Earl turned to his butler. "Cussin, you were on the stage?"

"Period of youthful experimentation, m'lord."

"And this man was your partner?"

"And his manager," Foreshadowing fingered his greasy bowler hat.

"Oh, I see," said the Earl. He pulled out his wallet and extracted two free coupons for Speedball Cola. "Sir, I am going to give you these coupons, and then you are going to depart this house and never return again."

"What's the cash value?"

"One centi-ha'panny."

"Is that so? And what if I disagree?"

"Then I shall have you arrested for pandering. Don't bother denying it, everyone knows what 'actor' is code for. And 'manager' as well."

Mr. Foreshadowing considered, then snatched the coupons from his lordship. Eyes burning, moustache in full attack posture, the little man spewed bile. "I'll take your coupons, but your lot won't always be on top! You'll see!" He pointed to the magazine he'd been reading, the one left by the little old ladies. "It's all in here! First there'll be a war, a long, loud, terrible war with the Germans—"

"Tell us something we aren't already preparing for," sniffed Wanna.

"—then, a period of general prosperity accompanied by changing mores. Shorter skirts, sexual liberation and lots of music by black people."

"I rather like the sound of that," Lady Unsybil said.

"Well, don't get used to it, because it will be followed by a great, great, economic collapse, where people will lose faith in the old power structure even further. Finally, there'll be another war with the Germans—"

"Two? With the same country? That's daft," Mr. Baits said.

"As may be, but it'll be even greater than the first one, and that conflagration will totally destroy this whole way of life. After all that, your lot'll be reduced to giving tours of your homes, just to pay the heat bill."

"That's all very interesting," the Earl said, "but can you boil it down for me? This scene's running a bit long."

Foreshadowing sighed. "Look, all I'm saying is, 'Watch out, gov! You'll be sorry someday!'"

"Not as sorry as you are now," Mr. Baits smirked. "Our dogsbody's just set fire to your motor."

"YOU GET AWAY FROM THERE!" He dropped the magazine and sprinted outside.

After Mr. Foreshadowing had gone, and the servants had dispersed, Lady Unsybil asked her father, "How did you know he would take the coupons?"

"I can spot the Speedball shakes from a mile away. Promise me you'll never touch the stuff."

"I promise, Papa," Lady Unsybil said, and went upstairs to hide her stash more carefully.

The Earl collected the nasty man's card from my tray and tore it neatly in half. (Would you think me crazy if I said that things torn in two always seemed to weigh more?)

Mr. Cussin looked up. "I suppose you'll be wanting my resignation, m'lord?"

"Nonsense, my good man. It will be much more fun to watch you wriggle every time the word 'songbird' comes up in conversation."

"Thank you, m'lord."

"Cussin, everyone has parts of their life they'd rather keep private."

"Too true, m'lord."

"Have I ever told you about 'Nelly Week' at Harrow?"

"No, m'lord."

"Or what I had to do to get my Blue for Oxford?"

"Please don't, m'lord. Let me retain my illusions."

"Or the summer I spent as a Sultan's concubine?"

"M'lord. I'm begging you—"

The Earl frowned. "Well, there's no need to be that way about it. Straight but not narrow, Cussin. Straight but not narrow."

• • •

The news of Mr. Cussin's mysterious past seeped through Downturn like the scent of Mrs. Phatore's cabbage. By the time Lady Violent came to visit a week later, it was common knowledge.

"You think you know a servant," Lady Cantswim said, "and then..."

"Each of us is a mystery to the other, Cola. Thank God." Violent sipped her tea and then said something her daughter-in-law was not expecting. "We must do something. Marry's randy enough to disrupt Fleet Week."

"Really, Violent!" She opened the teapot and sniffed. "What is in that tea?"

"Only the wisdom of decades. I'm not joking, Cola." Lady Violent continued. "I can see it in her eyes. She's a ticking time bomb."

"But what choice do we have? She's done four Seasons. The only men left are 'confirmed bachelors' like the Duke of Crowbar."

"Well, there is your solution."

"I don't understand."

"My dear woman, if Cussin can pass as a woman—and a twenty-stone one at that!—our Marry can surely pull off the reverse."

"In such a setting, one pretty girl could cripple the entire Empire."

"But Violent, I don't think people really thought—they knew that Cussin—"

"You give the masses too much credit. How very American of you." Lady Violent nibbled at a cake. "Marry could marry a man, one of these confused public-school chaps, and sort him out over time. The race must continue, you know. Or she could marry a woman, for all I care. The important thing is that she will be married and we can move on to the next plot-point."

"But—"

"Do you have a better idea?"

"No, but—"

"Then I suggest we fit Marry for a moustachio, before any more suitors get away."

Miss O'Lyin walked into the room. "Sorry to disturb, m'lady."

"Yes, O'Lyin, what is it?"

"It's for Lady Violent. Isapill Crawly and Dr. Clarkson are down in the village, conducting medicine."

"What? Those fools?" The old woman sprang up. "Tray-boy, fetch me my sword-parasol! And my pistol!"

•   •   •

"RIGHT!" Dr. Clarkson said, bracing his foot on the back of his new contraption; the guts of it were from a Dr. Osbert's Oscillating Pommel, but it had been souped-up considerably. A yank of the cord, and it sputtered to life with a mechanical clatter and a cloud of heavy smoke. "Hold her steady. We'll have her put right in a jiffy."

Ripping wasn't much of a town, and thus had to take what medical talent it was given. Dr. Clarkson was definitely light in that area, as he would cheerfully admit, but he tried to make up for it with an almost inhuman amount of brio. His colleagues at the hospital, Doctors May and Hammond, were equally clueless about medicine, but the three of them did put out a wonderful little broadsheet called *Topping Motors*, in which they described the latest in automobiles, and outlined their possible uses in medicine.

Doctors May and Hammond held Mrs. Fake down as their colleague advanced. The farmer's wife writhed, eyes wide at the oil-smeared gizmo in Clarkson's thick paws. Five feet away, Isapill Crawly crossed her fingers. "I pray it works," she said.

"Me too," Dr. May said, "otherwise we'll have to put her down!" It was all he could do to keep her pinned. "Hold still, woman! We're doctors!"

"Well, -ish," Dr. Clarkson said, polishing a bedknob pointlessly.

Dr. Hammond's wee form was slammed against the paneling. "Hurry up, will you? She's demolishing the bloody place!"

And she was: thirty-seven years of pent-up sexual frustration had turned the farmer's wife Mrs. Fake into some sort of mad creature. Dr. Osbert's Oscillating Pommel, the highlight of the 1874 World's Fair, and Queen Victoria's post-Albert consolation, was the woman's only hope.

Closer Dr. Clarkson came, closer and closer, until—

There was a strangely dainty gunshot.

"STOP!" Lady Violent's voice quavered bravely over the rudimentary two-stroke engine. "This woman must be left to die in peace!"

"She may die, but it won't be in peace, I can tell you that," Dr. Hammond said. "She's broken my finger."

The Dowager Countess turned to Mr. Fake. "And you? Do you want your wife to be publically humiliated like this?"

"If there's anyone here who should be humiliated, it is he," Mrs. Crawly sniffed. "Totally ignorant of female geography."

"She's right, m'lady. If my wife's to snuff it, at least she should go with a smile on her face."

"It's now or never," Dr. Clarkson asked, swiping the sweat from his beefy face. Their custom Pommel was a heavy little miracle.

Lady Violent placed her frilly pink gun down on my tray with a clatter. "On your heads be it."

"Give it the beans!" Dr. May said. "I don't know how much longer I can hold out!"

"POWERR-RRR!" Dr. Clarkson shouted, revving maniacally.

The device made contact, and half a minute later, Mrs. Fake was entirely transformed. The rigid-faced, clenching, angst-filled gorgon had been replaced by...

"...the woman I married," said the farmer, shedding tears of gratitude.

"John, we'll be taking that doohickey home with us," Mrs. Fake said, then she rolled over and went to sleep.

Fuming, the Dowager Countess stalked out, and I followed. As we exited the hospital, we saw Lady Marry canter by on her horse. A bushy brown moustache squatted aggressively on her delicate upper lip, like a caterpillar raping a rosepetal. Lady Violent murmured, "Suits her, don't you agree?"

Like any good tray-boy, I kept my mouth shut.

CHAPTER THREE.

You Will Meet a Tall, Dark, Stranger—Then Kill Him.
(November 1912-Monday, December 9, 1912)

One morning, Mr. Baits tapped me on the shoulder. "Percy, I need you to come with me down to the village."

"Sorry, Mr. Baits. Dhumbas says I have to stand here balancing this chamberpot until he gets back."

"Never mind about Dhumbas"—the valet lifted the full pot off my aching neck—"and count yourself lucky it isn't asparagus season. I've talked to Mr. Cussin. I'm picking up a parcel, and I need your help."

The trip down to Ripping took forever, him wincing and groaning with every step. About halfway there, Mr. Baits diverted to a small copse of junipers, and took out a small oil can. "Percy, if you don't mind, might you oil my chastity belt?"

"What's a chastity—oh my God." The valet dropped trou to reveal a mass of wood and metal plate encompassing him from belly-button to thigh. As was his wont, Mr. Baits wouldn't answer questions (I decided that he'd been shot by an Afrikaaner and needed it to hold his guts in), but we did make better time after the hinges turned freely. When we got to the P.O., the man behind the counter loaded our arms with packages. "That's twenty pounds black powder...Fuses, detonators, timers. Sign for it all here." The man had a moustache that began as nosehair, and just kept going. "Having a party up at the Abbey?"

"If this works," Mr. Baits said cryptically.

I was just about to ask him what he meant, when we bumped into Gwon, the housemaid. "Good morning, gentlemen."

"How goes the embodying of wide societal trends?" Mr. Baits' mood seemed to have brightened once we'd gotten the packages. His eye fell upon what Gwon was carrying. "What's under the handkerchief? Percy, do you have a guess?"

"Haven't a clue. A bird cage?"

Gwon laughed. "No, it's a test." She lifted the hankie, revealing a smooth ceramic head. "I'm learning Phrenology. From a correspondence course."

"Percy, let Gwon do you, for practice."

I removed my cap, and felt Gwon's long fingers play across my skull.

"Feels...flat," she said.

"Well then he's in the perfect profession."

On the walk back to Downturn, Gwon confided her excitement, and her doubts. "Some days, I think I'll never be able to leave service. My parents are so poor, my four sisters and I all have the same first name. So we could reuse the birth certificate."

"Percy here's got that beat. He's 'Percival Percival.'"

"What's your middle?"

"Take a wild guess," I said.

As we walked, Mr. Baits said seriously, "I think you'll make it, Gwon."

"That would be wonderful. What about you, Percy? Think I can do it?"

"Yes," I said. "Just don't fall in love, or smoke. Those types *never* leave."

.   .   .

Lady Cantswim walked into the sitting room where Lady Marry and Lady Edict were slap-fighting. "Where's Unsybil?" she asked.

"Out 'communing with nature,'" Lady Edict said. "Last I saw, she was banging her head against some tree and weeping."

"Mama, I think she's gone off the deep end," Lady Marry opined. "This morning, I caught her rubbing a rock under her armpits."

"Never mind that, Marry. I have some good news—Evelyn Staplier says he's coming for the hunt."

"EE-velyn, or his sister EV-elyn?" Lady Edict asked. "They have income, you'd think they'd spring for different names."

"Parents don't love all their children equally, hint-hint," Lady Marry said, opening a small gash under Lady Edict's left eye. "Anyway, I don't see how that's good news. Evelyn is boredom incarnate. All he talks about is office supplies."

"The whole family's like that." Lady Edict's finger dislodged Marry's moustache. "Do you remember when we went dancing there as children? Mrs. Staplier insisted on *collating* us. Oldest to youngest."

"Well, he's coming, girls, so make your peace with it. At the very least it will be a good chance to test out Marry's new disguise."

"But Mama, that's ridiculous. We've known each other since birth. He knows I'm a girl."

Her ladyship shrugged. "A man named 'Evelyn' has no room to press the point."

.   .   .

Having slalomed through the genial chaos of men, dogs, and horses that signals an imminent fox-hunt, I handed up a small glass of morning cheer to "Lord Marty."

33

"Thank you, Percy. You know, this is rather an improvement over side-saddle." And indeed there was a little extra color in her cheeks.

One of the beagles leapt up on a groom, raking him square across his gentleman's balls. Marry saw me laugh, so she did the same through her moustache. Then she punched the nearest man in the shoulder, inquired about a football match, and spat a gobbet on the ground. Finally she said loudly to no one in particular, "Fine morning for a hunt, what? A fine morning to kill a fox, and have testicles."

Lady Cola glided over. "Lord Marty—son—can I speak to you?"

"Cer-tain-ly," Lady Marry said, her voice sliding lower as she remembered.

"Been hitting the drinks horse rather early, haven't you?"

"Just trying to get into character, Mama."

"Well, pace yourself," her ladyship said. "You don't want to waste all your good material right at the start."

"I know, I know."

"I'm concerned you'll slip. Why don't you take Percy with you?"

"I'm not taking the tray-boy on a hunt! For one thing, he can't ride."

"It's all right. Percy, just wrap your arms around. Press down Lord Marty's twin incriminations."

I nodded. Even at eight, I realized that this was a plum assignment.

"If she makes a mistake, give her a tweak."

"Mama! That's quite out-of-bounds!"

The drinks horse (with collapsible gazebo). "The fox may escape, but you can always catch the drinks horse."—Saki.

"Do you want to get married, or don't you?" her ladyship turned, ending the conversation. "Ah! Evelyn!"

"It's Evelyn, actually," Mr. Staplier said, as I clambered up behind Lady Marry.

"That's right, Mama. EV-elyn's a girl's name, and there are no girls around here. Are there?"

"Apparently not," Mr. Staplier said. "Lord Marty, can I ask, how did this...

change come about?"

"Oh, you know, never been so very observant about such things," Lady Marry said. "After all, we're British."

"Yes." Mr. Staplier didn't quite see how that followed, but was not prepared to argue the point. He swiveled. "Here he is. Ladies—"

"Lady and gentleman," Lady Marry corrected.

"—may I introduce my friend, Mr. Carmel Galoot."

"How dreamy," Lady Cantswim said. "Wouldn't you agree?"

"I wouldn't have an opinion about that, Mama," Lady Mary said. "Being a masculine man of the male gender."

"But even men can recognize male beauty," Mr. Galoot said.

"*Ahem*—" Dhumbas handed up more sherry.

Lady Marry and Mr. Galoot drifted off together. "I say," Mr. Galoot murmured. "Terribly sorry I'm so disheveled."

"On the contrary, Mr. Galoot," Lady Marry said. "I find you perfectly sheveled—OW!"

(The tweak was a judgment call, but I felt the precedent had to be set.)

"My dear Marty, is there anything wrong?"

Lady Marry shook her head. "Thought I saw a small breach of etiquette, that's all."

"You English are so particular about your hunting. For you it is about pageantry. Costume. We Turks take our pleasure simply from the horse itself."

"Really," Lady Marry said. "Do go on."

"Amazing animal, the horse. Such power and beauty. And sensible, too."

"What do you mean?"

"It uses the same orifice for elimination and exquisite pleasure.[2] We humans could learn much—"

Then the horn sounded, and we were off.

• • •

Mr. Baits plucked the Earl's dinner jacket off my tray, and held it open. His lordship slid his arms in. "So what did you think of our guest?"

"Mr. Galoot, you mean m'lord?"

"Yes."

"I found it very restful. Not to be the center of amorous attention."

---

[2] Mr. Galoot was mistaken about this, as I later discovered to my profound personal regret.

"Yes, Baits, I've been meaning to ask you about that. You didn't seem to have this problem when we were in Africa."

"Well, I've grown much more tragic since then, m'lord. Not to mention mysterious."

Suddenly there was a tremendous explosion, epicentered six inches below Mr. Baits' waistcoat. Though the curtains cushioned me against the blast, the two men were thrown across the room, and blackened quite intensely with soot. Plaster fell from the ceiling like snow, and several pictures slid untidily to the floor.

The valet's voice issued weakly from somewhere near the armoire. "Oooh... that sucked."

"Baits!" the Earl said, clambering up from the rubble of his bedroom. "What is wrong? You *must* tell me!"

"It's nothing, m'lord." Mr. Baits caught a coatrack just before it fell to the floor. "Mrs. Phatore's cooking, perhaps."

"It's not nothing, man. Whatever you're doing is making the house quake several times a day. I know you love your privacy, but—"

"It's nothing," Mr. Baits said, and his definite tone put an end to it.

• • •

"But Unsybil, women already have the right to boat. I saw some on the water just yesterday."

"*Vote*, Granny, vote," Lady Marry corrected. "Mr. Galoot, can the ladies exercise the franchise in your country?"

"The sexes are strictly segregated in my country," said the dark visitor. "They cannot vote, or boat—but I like to think we give them plenty of exercise."

"Lucky them," Lady Edict said, as the footmen brought in another course.

"More food?" Mr. Galoot exclaimed.

"Just a bit of cheese and fruit to end the meal," Lady Cantswim said.

Mr. Galoot smiled. "Well, I had better pace myself, if I want to last the night."

"How was the hunt?" his lordship asked.

"Lovely," Lady Marry said. "Though I will surely feel it in the morning."

"It was invigorating," Mr. Staplier agreed. "Though you couldn't have told it by these two. Always lagging behind."

"We were looking for the drinks horse," Lady Marry said, "and got lost in the backcountry."

"Not lost. I prefer to hang back," the Turk said, "and attack from the rear."

Lady Edict fumbled her fork. "That's an interesting strategy."

"One unlikely to end fruitfully, if you don't mind my saying," Lady Violent sniffed.

"Lady Violent, sometimes encounters can be successful without being… fruitful."

All three Cantswim girls began fanning themselves vigorously, and even Lady Cantswim visibly tugged at her high-necked collar.

"Which one do I want?" Mr. Galoot took a red, ripe strawberry from the fruit platter. First, he licked it. Then he nipped it, just on the end, and gave a little moan. The table was transfixed, the men looking on in puzzlement, the women with a fascination of their own. Mr. Galoot rubbed the slightly opened berry all over his lips, so that the juice spilled redly on him; he seemed to be murmuring to it. Then, finally, when the table could stand no more, the suave foreigner devoured the berry, stem and all.

Lady Edict fell off her chair with a thump. No one noticed.

"Forgive me," said Mr. Galoot. "In my culture, we savor every bite."

"My, aren't other cultures fascinating?" Lady Marry said, flushed.

An uncomfortable silence hung until Mr. Crawly spoke. "That's nothing," he said, then pointed to Dhumbas. "You should see our footman eat a banana."

• • •

With all the servants living in close quarters, it was only a matter of time before someone discovered Gwon's practice head. Under the disapproval of Mrs. Snughes and Mr. Cussin, and the outright scorn of some nicotine-stained bad apples who shall not be named, Gwon's fragile confidence crumbled.

"It's no good!" Gwon wept. "I'll never get out of service! Phrenology will become a discredited pseudo-science!"

"Gwon, don't be silly," her roommate Wanna said, patting her softly. "You'll make it. I know you will."

"That's right," Mr. Baits said. "You're embodying a society-wide trend."

Gwon blinked away tears. "You really think so?"

"I know so."

"You can trust Mr. Baits," Wanna said. "He tells the truth. It's how he's been written."

"Except when he gives good news," I mumbled.

"Shhh! They'll stop reading!"

• • •

Marry had just drifted off to sleep when suddenly, silently, her bedroom door opened. There, clad in a silk peek-a-boo dressing gown, stood Mr. Galoot.

"Mister Galoot!" Marry scrambled for her moustache and pressed it to her lip. "Thank God you've come—I mean, what is the meaning of this?"

"I've felt this from the moment I saw you. We must be together!"

"I never, we mustn't, how dare you, my parents, blah blah blah—" Lady Marry flipped open the bedclothes. "Now get over here!"

Mr. Galoot snorted, then pawed the ground like a bull, once, twice. He dropped his dressing gown to reveal nothing but a prodigious banana-hammock in the Turkish national colors.

"My God..." Lady Marry gasped. The moustache slipped off her lip, fluttering to the bed like an etherized butterfly.

Mr. Galoot was similarly shocked. He pointed to the hirsute contrivance. "You—it—you're a woman?"

For a moment the two just stared at each other. "Oh well," Mr. Galoot finally said, "since I'm here..."

· · ·

"Wanna—Wanna, wake up!"

The housemaid woke to find Lady Marry's hand clasped tightly over her mouth. Lady Marry dragged her into the corridor. "What does it mean when you're doing it with a guy, and he goes 'Uhhh' and falls over, like?"

"That's pretty typical, sadly."

"Yes, but what if his eyes roll back in his head, and he gets a frightful expression?"

"Oh, m'lady, that just means you're doing it right."

"Yes, but what if after that, he gets all stiff?"

"Again? You thank your lucky stars!"

"No, no, you don't understand—" She pulled the housemaid down the corridor towards her bedroom. "You must help me!"

"All right, but sounds like you're doing just grand on your own..."

· · ·

They crept into Lady Marry's bedroom and closed the door. Wanna pulled her nightshirt over her head. "To whom will I owe the pleasure? Yes, turn the lamp on, it's fine with me—*what the blazes?*"

Wanna gawped at the inert Mohammedan. "Oh my God." The housemaid collected herself and turned to me. "Tray-boy," she said, "when two people love each other very much—"

"Forget about him, I'm in trouble!"

"You're not kidding. What the devil were you up to?"

"How should I know? No matter what Edict's told you, I've never done this before." Lady Marry said. "Things reached their conclusion, and when I returned to earth, he was dead."

"If it comforts you, I think he went on a high note," said Wanna, poking about.

"There's no need to paw him," Lady Marry said.

"I just wanted to see if it was true. What they say about Turkish gentlemen."

"Do 'they' also say they'll die? Because someone should bloody well tell you!"

I tried to be helpful. "Shall I wipe him down, m'lady? For fingerprints?"

Wanna shook her head. "I think it's too late for that."

"Then what shall we do?" Lady Marry asked.

"Percy, go downstairs and get the handtruck," Wanna said, all business. "The heavy metal one we use whenever a guest has had too much too drink. And look sharp—no one must see you. No one."

I got to the storage room and retrieved the handtruck without any trouble. But in the corridor leading to the back stairs, I ran into Craisy. She was crouched in the pre-dawn gloom, vainly trying to kindle a marble bust of Nelson.

"What are you doing awake-like?"

"Erm—sleepwalking!"

"That's all right then," she said. "I thought you were coming to stop The Great Work." (That's what the poor addled girl called her fires.)

"Wouldn't dream of it." I gave a snore, and hastened back to Lady Marry's.

When I returned, Lady Cantswim was there as well. I could tell by her expression that such situations were uncommon, even in America.

She pointed at me. "*He* knows too?"

"It's all right," Wanna said. "Percy's practically a mute."

"But he'll bankrupt us!" her ladyship exclaimed. "We'll have to buy his silence for eighty years!"

I felt a great flush of job security which I attempted to keep off my face.

"Oh, don't worry, Mama," Lady Marry said.

"Don't worry? Marry, are you mad?" Lady Cantswim checked herself. "What am I saying, of course you are! There's a dead wog in your bed!"

Wanna stiffened. "M'lady, that term is considered offensive."

"Not to me." A single tear slid down Lady Marry's cheek. "He'll always be my Well-Oiled Gentleman.'"

"Don't cry for him, daughter—cry for yourself. The shame! The scandal! You might even get pregnant!"

"Don't think we'll have to worry about that, m'lady," Wanna said.

Between quiet sobs Lady Marry dropped the final veil. "We used the servants' entrance."

CHAPTER FOUR.

A Twist of Fête.
(28 May - 6 June 1913)

None of us liked the new chauffeur. We didn't like his stringy hair, the nasty patchy scraggle that infested his chin, or the "staring contests" that always ended up with a member of the downstairs staff waking up naked and groggy out on the moors, covered in dried sheep's blood. Many's the day I'd shuffle downstairs to slip on my tray, and see some vacant-eyed village girl tapping at the backdoor in the weak morning light. "Is God at home?" "No, he is not. I expect you'll find him taking his wake-up tinkle out behind the stables." I don't know where he found those lost souls; maybe he put classifieds in *The Urchin*. But his lordship had hired him, for his lordship's reasons, and so we all put up with the chauffeur—even though the Earl himself would come round to our side of things eventually. But I'm getting ahead of my story.

I was there the day they met. His lordship was in the library, correcting the *Encyclopedia Brittanica*. "It's irresponsible, I tell you," he said, talking to me but not with me. "Twenty-three volumes and not one mention of fairies!"

There was a knock, and Mr. Cussin appeared. "The new chauffeur, m'lord."

"Ah, Manson," the Earl said. "Do come in."

"Thanks, man."

"Welcome to Downturn. Are you settling in all right?"

"What? Uh, yeah, man. I'm living out behind the stables, near some big trees, under the stars, man, next to Nature, killing what I eat, birds and squirrels, man. That's what people where meant to eat, not this plastic food. Plastic food makes plastic people, man, don't you see, don't you get it?"

"I...think so," the Earl said. "As long as you can drive members of the family—"

"The Family? Oh, man, Earl, I'd do anything for the Family. And they'd do anything for me. Because we're all connected, we're all One. There is no 'me,' there is no 'you.' One organism, man."

"I'm not sure I follow you, Manson."

Manson laughed. "That's all right, man. I respect that. I respect that you grok enough to grok what you don't grok. That's the first step. You see, Earl, dig: if I kill that silly kid standing next to you—"

"The tray-boy?"

"—if I did, maybe I put something real heavy on him, and squashed him flat, like a bug, I wouldn't really be killing him. I'd be killing myself. And who are the police, or the King, or anybody to tell me I can't kill myself? It's just me, man. Just me. Everything else is an illusion. Here, let me prove it to you..."

Manson took two steps towards me, and I looked nervously at the Earl.

"Now now, we mustn't injure Percy, you silly bugger," his lordship chuckled, "I paid a deposit." The Earl turned to me. "You can go, Percy." Then I heard his lordship reveal what had impelled him to bring this weirdo into our midst. "Now, Manson: on your application you spoke of having met the King of the Fairies. I wonder if you might corroborate some conclusions of my own regarding their governmental structure..."

As I left the room, I felt something on my neck; I looked back and there was the chauffeur, staring at me, opening and squinting his eyes in what I came to know as "his patented whammy." I showed him what I thought of it by shooting him a quick two-finger. Manson laughed malevolently, a sort of wheezy quiet *tee-hee-hee.*

The Earl turned. "Did you say something, Manson?"

"Asthma, man. All these dusty books." He laughed again.

It made my skin crawl. Manson had that effect.

•   •   •

With the young Mr. Crawly and Lady Marry not being an item, both her younger sisters began eyeing Downturn's presumptive heir with the same subtlety of aspect lionesses demonstrate in proximity to a wounded antelope. On this day Lady Edict, in her typically fun-loving way, had roped Mr. Crawly into a tour of the local churches—which Mr. Crawly, in his typically mercenary way, had turned into a sort of imaginative bazaar.

"Does this church come with the Earlship/Earldom/Earlitude/whatever?"

"I don't think so, no," Lady Edict said.

"Bit chinzy, don't you think? Still, there must be something...That's a nice window."

"Yes, it's from the 15th century."

"Crikey, sounds valuable. Think they'd miss it?"

"They'd notice the breeze immediately. Cousin Dratyew, please get down from there."

"Just seeing how it was attached."

"Quite, but I wouldn't want you to dash out your brains," Lady Edict said, though the more time she spent with Mr. Crawly, the less passionately she felt about it.

"Hello—how about these candlesticks?"

"Oh, please put those down."

"Why?" Mr. Crawly opened his jacket, snuggling the glittering item against his ribcage. "They'd fit perfectly. Nobody'd be the wiser."

Lady Edict got a slightly wild-eyed look; since we were alone, he might actually do it. She pointed at me. "*He* would know! The tray-boy would tell."

"Who, Percy? He can't speak."

"I can, m'lord," I said. "I simply choose not to."

"Amazing," Mr. Crawly said. "Well, I must make some profit on this venture." Lady Edict grabbed a tattered *Book of Common Prayer*, and thrust it forward. "Here, take this! It's worth a fortune!"

"Interesting." He turned it over in his hands. "Hiding in plain sight, very cunning. How much do you think I could get?"

"Twenty pounds—no, a hundred! It's terribly rare! I'll give you a hundred pounds for it!" Lady Edict was frightfully desperate to get out of the church without stealing any of God's stuff.

"Well, I think you're getting the worse of the deal, but sold."

"Thank Christ...I mean, pleasure doing business with you."

Mr. Crawly sauntered down the aisle towards the exit, whistling. "I warn you Cousin Edict: I fully expect you to come across once we get back to Downturn."

The girl's heart leapt. "Really?"

"Yes, I'm not leaving without a cheque."

Lady Edict shot me a look of pure deflation and disgust. I shrugged silently, but not unsympathetically. In-breeding is a terrible thing.

• • •

Upstairs at Downturn, romance was constantly in the air, which isn't so surprising given the primarily commercial nature of upper-class matrimony; everyone has to make a living. More worthy of note were the times the lovebug meandered belowstairs. Like, for example, the day I spotted Mrs. Snughes down in Ripping, taking in the delights of the village fair in the company of a mysterious gentleman.

As you've surely realized already, respecting people's privacy is a signal virtue of mine, a sacred obligation almost, and so under normal circumstances I would've never watched them in secret. Nor would I have hastened back to the great house to put on an exuberant dramatic rendition for the others. It's just that the man seemed so familiar to me—and it was the first time I'd seen Mrs. Snughes fully awake.

"So the bloke in the pointy helmet had his mitts on Mrs. Snughes' bubbies," Dhumbas said. "What happened next?"

"I think we can surmise what happened next," sneered Miss O'Lyin. "No one goes to The Slap and Tickle except that wants to indulge in depraved carnality."

"Yes, but what sort of depraved carnality? Percy, demonstrate."

Downturn's pair of bad eggs sniggered unkindly as I rolled around on the floor, miming first the gentleman, then our colleague thus—and thus—and thus.

Dhumbas laughed. "I do believe he's seen that before."

I froze—did they know of Lady Marry and the Turk?

"The boy exaggerates," Miss O'Lyin said. "She was never so limber."

"I think he's telling the truth," Dhumbas said.

"And I think he's been at those picture postcards of yours."

Miss O'Lyin was right; I been embellishing wildly for at least the last seven positions. But before I could stammer out a denial, the fearsome figure of Mr. Cussin filled the doorway. "Dhumbas, Miss O'Lyin, I realize our modern era rewards slacking, but as far as I am aware, corrupting the tray-boy is not part of your duties. Percy, why are you on the floor twisted up like a pretzel?"

"He had a fit," Dhumbas said.

"Entertainment's where you find it," Miss O'Lyin said defiantly.

"So said Jack the Ripper," Mr. Cussin frowned. "All three of you, get back to work."

• • •

But such gymnastics, as unseemly as they might have been on the part of Mrs. Snughes, were leagues more wholesome than what was taking place, day by day, in the Cantswim's auto. Upon hearing that Lady Unsybil was "interested in politics," Manson the chauffeur had embarked upon nothing less than a full indoctrination.

His Ladyship's youngest had always been a bit susceptible, but under the dubious care of Mr. Manson, her gentle ways were being molded in bizarre new directions.

"So Manson, who exactly are 'the pigs' again? I keep forgetting."

"Anybody in authority— the King, the man who runs the tea shop, this McVitie on the biscuit tin—"

Manson immediately began customizing the family car. "These headlamps look right into your soul, man."

"And we are supposed to 'off' them, is that correct?"

"Sure, man. To save them from themselves."

"Right. And what happens after that?" Lady Unsybil asked. "Sorry I'm so dim, Manson, it's just that growing up with privilege, as I have, the real world you're telling me about can be a bit, well, 'far-out.'"

"It's cool, man."

"So what's the big brouhaha you mentioned before? What's that called?"

"Uh…" For once, Manson was at a loss for words. I saw him glance out of the window at a ride that had been erected on Ripping Green. "Helter Skelter," he said. "That's what it's called."

"And how did you come to know all this, Manson? Through Papa's library?"

"Sure," Manson said. "Plus secret messages."

"Secret? How glamorous!"

"Yeah, secret messages from—" Manson looked out again, and spied a group of musicians practicing for this evening's concert. "—those guys over there."

"The raggedy fellows with the long hair and mustaches?" Lady Unsybil gawped. "How remarkable. I must say, Manson, the day you came to work for us was a lucky one indeed."

"I feel the same way," he said. I coughed, and Manson shot me a dirty look.

•　•　•

Though the rides were as lethal as always, the traveling fair ended without violence, no thanks to Manson and his young acolyte. After an enjoyable, but tiring evening,

I was on duty in Mrs. Snughes' office, two glasses of wine on my head.

"So Mrs. Snughes, will you be leaving us?" Mr. Cussin asked.

"Bill is a lovely man, underneath all the bluster," she said tenderly, "and he would take good care of me. Did I tell you that he gave me a colony in Africa?"

"A whole colony?"

"A small one. Still, no paramour has ever done that before."

"So why not leave? Devotion has its limits."

Mrs. Snughes sighed. "Tell that to Bill. He's always working. Not that he doesn't have a reason, being in charge of Germany and all…I'm afraid that, when it comes down to it, I'll always be second-best."

"Well, I'm glad we'll still have you," Mr. Cussin said, "and I hope it's the right decision. Was Mr. Kaiser angry when you told him?"

"Oh frightfully angry, Mr. Cussin. He sounded just like you, only in German!" They laughed. "Bill walked away swearing blue murder. 'I'll start a war against England, then you'll see!' I tried to tell him that bombing where I live, and killing my countrymen wasn't the way to my heart, but by that time he was off into one of his moods. There's no reasoning with him when he's like that." Mrs. Snughes yawned. "My word, one sip of wine!…I'd go with him if I thought he was serious. I wouldn't want to be the cause of any trouble."

"Men have a tendency to exaggerate, Mrs. Snughes, especially in matters of the heart. Time has a way of healing such things. I don't think he'll actually do it."

"If you're sure…"

"I *am* sure. Percy, Mrs. Snughes is sleepy. Let's help her to her room."

"Oh, you don't have to…"

"Indeed we do," Mr. Cussin said. "Lord knows where you'll drop otherwise. Having you lying about is a definite fire hazard."

"Mr. Cussin, Bill Kaiser isn't the only sweet man in Ripping."

"I'm glad you think so. Percy, grab her things; I'll carry her fireman's style."

CHAPTER FIVE.

Does M'lord Prefer the Prince of Wales Kush,
or the Sour Cheltenham O.G.?
(31 July - 9 August 1913)

By a happy chance of geography and climate, the area around Downturn Abbey was that part of England most favorable for growing certain plants of a mildly narcotic and pleasantly hallucinogenic nature. In addition to explaining why the local population put up with centuries of the inept Cantswims at their head, this fact also led to a tradition particular to Ripping: the annual Herb Show.

Since the Show's establishment by Robber's father, the fifth Earl of Cantswim and former Viceroy of Jamaica, the Best of Show cup had been regularly won by Lady Violent, who insisted that her use was strictly medicinal. "I have glaucoma! I have the megraine!"

"You mean you *give* the megraine," the Earl griped, inspecting a table groaning with foliage. "What's this one called again, Mr. Marley?"

"Let me see—is that the Dirty Bertie or the Prince of Wales Kush?" The wizened old man trundled around to the front of the table, brushing his gray dreads out of his eyes. "I'm wrong, it's neither. That's the Elephant and Castle Sour Diesel. Strong stuff. One can expect quite a bit of divan-lock."

"What about the munchies?" asked Lady Unsybil.

"And how do you know about 'munchies,' young lady?" her ladyship demanded. "Bloody Skeltons."

"I have the megraine! Like Granny!"

Mr. Marley smiled. "It do run in families." As Lady Violent's annual competition, he was the source of some of her headaches.

Isapill Crawly said, "Mr. Marley, I'm glad to see my old friend 'Sour Cheltenham O.G.'" She was no stranger to his wares; whenever he'd come over to visit his son, the Crawly's butler, he'd leave something behind. "It makes one so delightfully peaceful. We should send some to Germany." She turned to Lady Violent, who was examining Marley's table with a gimlet eye. "It's like riding the back of a pink velvet dolphin through a warm lavender sea."

"What a revolting image," the Dowager Countess carped, and skulked away.

• • •

When her ladyship strided into the library the next morning, my immediate thought was, she certainly could certainly use some Sour Cheltenham O.G. Unfortunately, all she had was the dubious comforting powers of her husband, who was working on his fairy engine. This was a means of power production that harnessed the wee people. One could not say that the Earl was not a visionary. Or something.

"Robber, put down that balsa doodad, we have to talk."

"Now stay still, Percy..." The Earl placed the tiny treadmill upon my tray. "Yes, dear, what is it?"

"Our daughter Marry!" Her ladyship waved a letter angrily. "Your sister Rosibuns says there's a rumor floating around London regarding her character!"

"Whose character, Rosibuns or Marry's?" the Earl asked. "You really need to write better sentences."

"Be serious, Robber—why would I care about your sister's character? Everyone knows that Rosibuns Swifkick is a world-class roundheel. But Marry, she needs to get married."

"So what is this dreaded rumor, that will surely ruin our daughter for ever and ever?"

"That she is afflicted with the Curse of Nefertiti."

"Oh pish," Lord Cantswim said. "You and I both know that all Cousin Jerk found in Egypt was paternity suits."

"Perhaps, but it would be a lot easier to refute if Jerk were around to help." Several years ago, the Earl's ill-fated cousin had headed an archeological expedition to Egypt, looking for the final resting place of Nefertiti, Queen of the Nile. Lord Jerk's team of boffins found the tomb all right, but when it was clear there were no cartloads of gold forthcoming, his lordship's attention wandered and he decamped for Blighty, taking the funding with him.

"You don't honestly believe in it, do you?"

"Of course not," Lady Cantswim said. "I think those frightful dusty rascals made the whole story up, just to get back at Jerk. But now poor Marry must go around with everyone thinking that whomever she sleeps with, dies."

"Luckily there is no proof of that."

"Haha yes," Lady Cantswim laughed nervously.

"Well, I see only two courses before us," his lordship said, really wanting to get back to his fairy engine. "Either let every suitor take Marry out for 'a lap around the track,' or—"

"Forgive me, Robber—O'Lyin, have you been standing there the entire time?"

"I was just...lurking, m'lady."

"Well, stop it. And take Percy with you."

• • •

Five minutes later, I was on ashtray duty in the back stairwell. Wreathed in blue smoke, Downturn's bad apples were rubbing butter on each step, just where Mr. Baits might put his cane.

"It's not that I don't want to cause trouble; I do," said Dhumbas. "But there's no percentage in this one."

"Unlike sinking the *Titanic*, you mean?"

"Very funny. Look, if Lady Marry doesn't wed, the Cantswims will have to sell Downturn."

"So?" Miss O'Lyin said. "They aren't kin to me, or you neither. I happen to think a little suffering might be good for them."

"Think, you silly bugger: if they go, we'll be sacked. No sane family would put up with our shenanigans. I just don't see the benefit."

"So now we're supposed to make sense? None of these schemes ever help us, not really. But we do them anyway, because we're evil. *EEEEE-vil!*" Miss O'Lyin's laughter echoed eerily throughout the stairwell. Eventually Dhumbas gave in and started laughing, too.

Craisy entered the stairwell two floors below. Hearing the laughter, she dropped her bucket and cried, "Jesus, Mary and Joseph! It's haunted!"

"Craisy! Just the girl we wanted to see!" Dhumbas ground his butt out on my head, and sprinted down the stairs after her. Until he slipped on the butter. "Bloody hell!"

Smiling, Miss O'Lyin looked at him hanging off the banister. "Works a treat, don't it?"

• • •

The explosion—small, but an explosion nevertheless, and nearby—woke Mrs. Snughes. As grumpy as a hibernating bear, she stumbled in the direction of the blast, rubbing her eyes, determined to find out why and what for.

There was Mr. Baits, laying in the ruins of the china cabinet. The table had been knocked on its side; his face was scorched and blackened, and his trousers above the knee hung in scorched tatters. "Got to get it off..." he mumbled.

"My word, Mr. Baits, are you hurt? And what is that contraption around your party bits?"

"It's a chastity belt...homemade..." Mrs. Snughes helped him into a chair.

"I can see that," she said. It was a mass of plates and spikes and fine wires, quite nasty to behold. "I can also see why it's been so painful for you to walk. Why on Earth do you wear it?"

"Mrs. Snughes, have you ever been married?"

"No."

"Then you wouldn't understand."

"Try to explain anyway."

"Well," Mr. Baits said, "every man, when he gets married, puts one of these on, and gives the key to his wife, who stores it for safekeeping. The wife does the same. Each one handmakes the device for the other. It's an old tradition of the Church, but no one tells anyone about it because it must be secret in order to work."

"I see. And who told you this?"

"My wife. Well, ex-wife. Well, it's complicated."

"Everything with you always is," Mrs. Snughes sighed. "But that's why we love you. Now, Mr. Baits, I'm afraid your wife—"

"Genghis."

"How appropriate. Genghis told you a bit of a fib."

"I thought she may have," Mr. Baits said sadly.

"Where is your wife now? More importantly, where is that key?"

"I don't know. I am trying to divorce her."

"I can understand why! And all the black powder—"

"Trying to blow it off."

"I see." Mrs. Snughes stood up, dusting herself off. "Will you help me clear this up?"

"Of course."

"And can we declare that method a failure?"

"I suppose so."

"There'll be other ways to punish yourself unfairly, Mr. Baits, I promise you. Life has a way of providing them."

"I know it does, Mrs. Snughes. For example, I seem to have part of a butterdish stuck in my bottom."

•   •   •

Lady Edict was hard at work, writing a letter to *The Times*, suggesting that David Lloyd George had "half a stone of undigested chewing gum in his stomach." She was pondering whether chewing gum was hyphenated or not, when there was a knock at the door.

It was Miss O'Lyin, looking as luscious as a bramble bush, and with Downturn's smoke-scented dogsbody in tow. "I've brought Craisy to you, m'lady."

"Ah. Thank you, O'Lyin. You may go." Lady Edict got up and walked over to her bed. "Craisy, come sit here."

"Yes, m'lady." She sat on the edge; soft things weren't meant for poor people.

"Now, Craisy, Miss O'Lyin told me that you might have something nasty to reveal about my sister. Is that true?"

"I shouldn't like to say, m'lady."

"Craisy, do you have sisters?"

"I did, m'lady. But I had to eat them when I was in the womb."

"Heavens! Then you know how it is. Sisterhood is not pleasant, Craisy."

"No 'tisn't, m'lady."

"But you see, people like us, Craisy, people of the upper classes—we cannot simply consume each other. There would be quite a scandal."

"No, m'lady."

"We must fight it out in other ways. If you tell me whatever it is that you know about Lady Marry, I will give you this lovely frock."

"But when would I wear it?"

Lady Edict paused. "All right, then," she said. "if you tell me, I will let you *set fire* to this lovely frock."

"Ooh, m'lady—but I shouldn't like to tell. Too much of Season One hinges on my bad judgment as it is."

"But surely that's not your fault, is it now, Craisy?" Edict said. "Surely you just act as you are written, just like the rest of us."

"I still don't think I should."

"Damn it, girl! Don't you see that it's better for all concerned for you to tell me? Otherwise, I'll have to try harder and harder to defeat my sister and, who knows where that will end? World War, perhaps."

"You're crazy," Craisy declared.

"Am I? Our King, the Czar of Russia, and Kaiser Wilhelm of Germany are all cousins. This War that's coming—whatever the history books will say caused it—I wager one of them had a dogsbody who screwed up!"

Craisy brightened. "How about I tell you another secret instead? It's good."

Lady Edict studied her cuticle. "Whatever."

"The Kaiser met Mrs. Snughes down at the Fair, and asked him to come away with her. But she refused. She couldn't bear not having Cook's famous potpies every Friday evening," Craisy said. "I don't like them, myself. I've seen Cook make them." Craisy leaned over and whispered. "They're *people*. Cook gets the bodies from Sir Antony Strangler."

"Who's crazy now?" Lady Edict scoffed. "You may go."

The dogsbody got up. "Thank you, m'lady." She paused at the door. "Sorry I couldn't tell you about Lady Marry."

Lady Edict wondered, did the lower orders feel guilt? She decided to chance it. "If twenty millions die as a result of this feud between my sister and I," Lady Edict said, "I'll bet you'll feel pretty sorry then. Think about that, Craisy."

•   •   •

On the day of the Ripping Herb Show, the household staff finished their duties as early as possible, so they could make the short trek down to the village in time for the judging. As the others pulled ahead, Mr. Baits took the opportunity to confess to Wanna.

"...so that is why I can't walk faster," Mr. Baits said. "I hope you don't think less of me."

"Less of you, no," Wanna said. "Less fun at parties, yes. But why did you do it, Mr. Baits? Why did you lock your manhood away?"

"A woman that I once loved said it was a family tradition and, young fool that I was, I believed her."

"So there's some poor unfortunate lass who is strapping dynamite to *her* nethers as well? That might be a comfort if it weren't so incredibly...stupid."

"It gets worse," Mr. Baits said. "After I got into mine, and gave her the key, she didn't get into hers."

"How awful for you. How unfair."

"And I got a butter dish lodged in my bottom."

"I'm not going to ask. Mr. Baits, are you going to continue to try to get free? Please say yes."

"I will, but I don't expect to succeed," Mr. Baits said. "Wanna, you'd do well to forget me. Forget me, and this tin-and-chicken wire prison of my own creation."

"And do what? Moon after Dhumbas? I'd have to grow a moustache first. Killem? Everyone knows he's not long for this world. Manson? Mr. Cussin? I'm sorry, Mr. Baits—I'm a desperate woman. I don't care what I have to do, or how long it takes. We're going to break your bollocks out of jail. *Together.*"

•   •   •

Craisy peered into the window at the throng gathered inside. "And the winner of the 1913 Best in Show cup is..." Who cares? Craisy thought, as the crowd erupted into cheers. Let them chase after trifles. Let them squabble and struggle— it would keep them busy, distracted, so that she could continue her Great Work.

Quietly, crouching down so that no one could see, Craisy crept around the building, sprinkling paraffin around the foundation.

"Hey, you—what do you think you're doing?"

"Nothing, Dr. May!" In one fluid, exquisitely practiced motion, Craisy struck a match and dropped it onto the paraffin.

"Bloody Nora!" Dr. May yelled as Craisy ran. She watched from a safe distance as the crowd tumbled out. No one was hurt in the least, there was plenty of time—but not so much that the building could be saved. The structure, and all the entries in the Cup, went up in smoke.

This quantity was quite incredible in its effects; no one within a thirty-mile radius of Ripping escaped un-mellow. Social orders mixed as never before, denizens bonding over life's glorious wonder or, if unlucky, crushing anxiety/paranoia.

In her secret hideaway fifty yards from the Biblical column of grooviness towering into the bright blue sky, Craisy sprawled, giggling at her handiwork. Suddenly, she found herself circling the same thought over and over, but not minding it overmuch. Was it true that Dhumbas shaved his goolies, and how would Mrs. Phatore know that?

She'd just asked herself that question for the six hundredth time when Lady Edict appeared in the gully beside her. "M'lady! How long have you been there?"

"Some..." Lady Edict said languidly. "I've just been...looking at...this leaf."

"Can I ask you a question, m'lady?"

"Only if I can ask you one."

"Does Dhumbas the footman shave his twiddle-diddles?"

"His what?"

"His talleywags."

Lady Edict's look remained blank.

"His trinkets. His whirlygigs. His thingamabobs. His *BALLS*."

"Yes," Lady Edict guessed. After they were both done giggling, she tried to make her face go serious. Which made them giggle more. Finally she got the words out somehow. "Now my question: what do you know about Lady Marry?"

Craisy squirmed—outfoxed again! If only she could think, perhaps a suitable lie would come. But it was fruitless. In a slow, meandering, confusing, endlessly repetitive way, the girl spilled Lady Marry's terrible secret.

• • •

I was there in Lady Edict's room when she wrote the letter. We went through a whole trayful of pens—she was pressing so hard, so gleefully, that her nib splintered every fifteen words. "Dear *Naughty Ladies Magazine*," she began. "I never thought I'd be writing a letter like this. But then my slutty sister joined giblets with a Turkish chap staying at our house…"

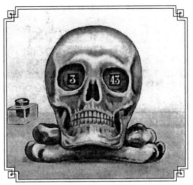

We all hated Manson's dashboard clock.

CHAPTER SIX.

"It's Always 1851 at Vicky and Bert's!"
(May 1914)

Wedged malevolently in the front seat of the car, Manson was livid. "Oh he'll suffer. They all will, man...Their day is coming, sooner than they think! They think I'm the criminal, but I'm not the criminal! They're the criminals, man!" Twitching with agitation, Manson glowered at a small fellow standing on the sidewalk, then screamed so hard his chauffeur hat fell off. *"Bourgeois hypocrite pig!"* The inocuous object of his fury flinched, dropping his ice cream.

"Oh, Manson, don't be like that, he just crossed in the middle." Lady Unsybil looked out the back window, smiling at all the activity on Ripping's High Street. This was her favorite time of the week. On Friday and Saturday evenings, all of the local gentry's younger children gathered in Ripping to "cruise." Their chauffeurs would drive them up and down the boulevard for hours, so they could trade gossip, throw visiting cards through open windows, see who was wearing what and dating who.

"Oooh! Cecilia!" Lady Unsybil blew a kiss to a girl she knew from dances at the Stapliers.

"Love your car!" Lady Cecilia said.

"Yours is awesome," Lady Unsybil said.

"I say, Unsybil, fancy a bit of grub at Vicky and Bert's?"

"I'd love it—Manson, follow that yellow Austin."

"I know the way to Vicky and Bert's," Manson grumbled. "It's at the corner of Bourgeois and Pig."

"Don't get uptight," Lady Unsybil said. "Percy and I will bring you some dinner." Vicky and Bert's was a theme restaurant that had just opened, but was already the clear favorite among the younger set. Everything, from the décor to the menu, was meant to recall a time fifty years earlier—and if there were slight historical hiccups here and there, such as a mechanical cash register, Speedball Cola, and toilet paper in the lav—no one minded much.

"Why not eat in the car?" Manson said.

"Have some sympathy for your fellow workingman, Manson. The poor waiters have to bring the food out on those dreadful bicycles with the big front wheel. By the time it gets to you, half of it's all over the road."

Lady Unsybil took me with her, so I could make notes; that way the gossip could flow freely and she would not be hindered by the details. "I just love this place," she said as we slid into a booth. "So cozy and restful. The past was ever so much less difficult, don't you think? Things made sense then, not like today..."

"But m'lady, back in those days, you wouldn't be out of an evening. And milkshakes hadn't even been invented."

"I know, I know, Percy—I don't want to *live* back then, just...pretend." She scanned the menu. "What'll you have?"

The prices were outrageous. "Just gruel, I guess."

"Nonsense! Two Fashoda-Burgers! My treat."

As Lady Unsybil stared out the window looking for Cecilia's car, she saw a group of young men sidle up to the entrance. They were dressed in the most peculiar way, like Arthurian knights outfitted by Mrs. Phatore. The motley assortment boasted tablecloth tunics with shaky stitching, mop handle pikes, and shields made of serving trays. Once inside, they dispersed, distributing slips of paper.

"Tournament on the Village Green, next Saturday," a spotty-faced champion mumbled, sticking the flyer between our cruets.

A waiter in an apron hurried out from the kitchen. "You young rascals can't come in here, your nostalgia's clashin' with ours!"

"But—" Before the kid could say another word, the waiter had grabbed him by his scruff and breastplate (a ladies' corset turned around) and tossed him into the street. There was vague talk of "defending honor," but one look from the waiter was enough to rout his compatriots. "...and don't call me 'varlet,' either!"

Lady Unsybil looked at the slip of paper, interested to see what could cause such a reaction.

"Are they really holding a joust?" I asked.

Before Lady Unsybil could respond, Lady Cecilia, a slightly blotchy dishwater blonde who will not appear again in this story, plopped herself down. "All those frightful boys in their outrageous outfits. Do you know, one of them had a colander on his head? What era do they think we're nostalgic for, anyway?"

"I rather dig them," Lady Unsybil said, handing me the flyer for safekeeping. I noed with displeasure her adoption of Manson's peculiar argot. "Percy, would you like a General Gordon Milkshake? They're far-out."

.   .   .

The next day, I was doing my duty in the morning room, and staring at the boys' flyer during a quiet moment. I had just about puzzled out what "Creative Anachronism" meant when the door opened, and a very alarming gentleman strided in.

"Sir Antony Strangler," Mr. Cussin intoned.

To call the visitor's appearance "alarming" makes a mockery of our mother tongue. It wasn't that he was roughly dressed, or out-of-date; quite the opposite in fact. In that which he could control, Sir Antony was a perfect gentleman. But in that which he could not—in that which he *was*, from his beady, darting eyes to the cruel curl of his lip, to the restless, sudden pair of hands that seemed to long to squeeze—he was not so much man as animal. Even his speech flowed in a peculiar rhythm that was hard to follow, sometimes smooth and cultured, other times bestial, almost howling.

"Good morning, ladies," Sir Antony lisped. "Lady Cantswim, I would like to invite your daughter Lady Marry to a—" Suddenly, he took one step to the side, and canted his head down, as if he were talking to himself. "MURDER!"

He slapped his own face. "Forgive me. I meant to say, 'a very special engagement.'"

Lady Cantswim smiled. "Can you tell us what kind of engagement?"

"ARE YOU A COPPER?" Slap. "Er, I'd rather keep it a surprise."

Her ladyship made a quick calculation—she could not afford to be picky. "Well, can you give us a hint?"

"I have a new car. I should like to take Lady Marry in it—" "AND SLAUGHTER HER LIKE A HOG!" Slap. "And take her for a drive. Please say no. I'm begging you!"

"I see," said Lady Marry, not seeing at all. "Would dinner be involved?"

"NOT FOR YOU!" "No! Shut up! Shut up! Let me alone, will you?"

"I have a feeling we are intruding," Lady Violent said, to no one in particular.

"Well, I'm sorry, Sir Antony, but I'm afraid I'm busy. Do call again."

"Thank god." The relief that flooded Sir Antony's face creased into a mask of pure sadism. "NO! NO! SHE MUST!" He pounded his temples so furiously I thought he was going to knock himself down. "THE REST ARE TOO SMALL!"

Lady Edict cleared her throat, then asked tentatively, "Would you take me?"

The beating stopped. Sir Antony glared at Lady Cantswim's middle daughter. "ALL...right," he said, voice changing mid-sentence. "I shall pick you up next Wednesday. Please, by all that is right and holy, prepare yourself."

Lady Violent was the first to speak after Sir Antony had departed. "Next to him, Manson is a dream date."

"We mustn't be too hard on the poor man," Lady Cantswim said, showing the same instinct for people that kept Miss O'Lyin employed. "It's because his wives have died."

"All five of them," Lady Marry said.

"The poor dear has no conception of how to take care of himself. Some men are like that," her ladyship said, "until they find the right girl."

"I should be delighted to go driving with him," Lady Edict said.

Lady Marry snorted. "It's your funeral."

• • •

I was worried for Lady Edict, but that night big doings belowstairs made me forget about everything, even Mr. Strangler. We were all in Mr. Cussin's office. On the one side of Mr. Cussin stood Miss O'Lyin and Dhumbas; on the other, Mr. Baits and Wanna.

"So, Miss O'Lyin, Mr. Baits did something naughty. What was it?"

"I shouldn't like to say, Mr. Cussin."

"So you're accusing him, but you will not say of what?"

"That's right," Miss O'Lyin said, "he knows what he did. Have him tell it."

"Mr. Baits, can you shed any light on this?"

"I did not do it."

"Do what?"

"I'm sorry, Mr. Cussin"—Mr. Baits' eyes twinkled with the knowledge he was tormenting milions of viewers—"but I'm not at liberty to say."

Downturn's butler let out an explosive burst of profanities, for once having nothing to do with a supposed decline in standards. "I have dealt with British people all my life, and a certain opacity is to be expected. Discretion, a phlegmatic nature, it can be part of their charm! But this—how am I supposed to function?" He turned to the valet. "Just tell me this: Is Miss O'Lyin lying?"

"Yes," Mr. Baits said, "and no."

"Elucidate, you cipher!"

"She isn't being truthful, true," Mr. Baits said, "but there is truth in what she says."

"What? Can you explain?"

"No."

"Why not?"

"It would not be right—"

Mr. Cussin cut him off. "Miss O'Lyin? Please, I'm begging you." (Mr. Baits continued skeining out rationales as the rest talked.) "How about you, Dhumbas? Do you know?"

"Haven't a clue," the first footman said. "I think he's barmy."

"Wanna, he likes you—can you tell what Mr. Baits is on about?"

"No. But isn't it *dreamy*?"

* * *

Upstairs, Mr. Cussin's torments went unnoticed. They had other fish to fry—as I was to witness the very next morning, when Lady Violent charged into the solarium. The gust from her entry was more than enough to topple her ladyship's matchstick Parthenon. "Why, you desiccated old—"

"Never mind that! Cola, I've just received the most disturbing letter from my friend Lady Flintstone."

"'Friend' is a bit excessive, don't you think? The Flintstones walk around in animal skins."

"That is nothing compared to what she is accusing my granddaughter of!"

"Oh, no one takes Edict's letters seriously. She just wrote Gregorii Rasputin pretending to be an old lady with piles."

"It's not Edict I'm talking about. It's Marry." The Dowager Countess pulled out the letter, positioned her lorgnette, and began to quote the seamier portions. "Hugging, kissing...'Fluff-diving'? What is 'fluff-diving'? Flintstone has the most terrible handwriting...It goes on for pages! 'Rusty trombone'? 'Dirty Sanchez'? Don't tell me a foreigner was involved." Lady Violent battled the vapors. "Cola, what do you have to say to this? Is any of it true?"

Lady Cantswim didn't answer.

"Some of it?"

Lady Cantswim didn't answer.

"All of it?"

Lady Cantswim didn't answer.

"Ye gods!" Lady Violent swooned into a chair. "The little fool! Such activities are only necessary for girls *without* dowries." She fanned herself for a moment, then jabbed her wizened finger at a sentence. "And, though I am afraid to ask, what does Lady Flintstone mean by 'Yabba Dabba Doo'?"

"That I can't help you with. Percy, get a dustpan for my Parthenon."

• • •

With scenes like that, it was almost a relief to go out driving with Lady Edict and Sir Antony—almost. When his lordship had heard about the plan, the only way he'd allow Edict to go was if I accompanied her, ostensibly to be a trail chair, but in reality with a hypodermic full of thorazine in case Sir Antony got out of hand.

Now the three of us were speeding through the countryside, nobility in the frontseat, and myself in the back, syringe at the ready.

"You know, they say inside every man is a woman fighting to get out," Sir Antony said.

"Who said that?"

"My late wife, God rest her soul. So kind, so trusting. She never realized—"

"What was your wife like?"

"LESS ROOMY THAN SHE LOOKED!"

Though trained in the art of conversation, Lady Edict was momentarily thrown. "Uh...I admire your driving gloves."

"They're of my own manufacture." "YOU CAN SAY THAT AGAIN!"

"Really? How talented. Perhaps you could make me a pair."

"I'LL MAKE YOU INTO MORE THAN THAT!"

"What?"

"HOW SUSCEPTIBLE ARE YOU TO ETHER?"

"As much as the next girl, I suppose."

"Oh, god, I pray there won't have to be a next girl."

Lady Edict blushed. Could it be true?

"JUST KEEP EATING, AND DON'T SKIMP ON THE LOTION!"

That's when I hit 'im with the hypodermic. Lady Edict was absolutely furious with me, but she did enjoy driving us back home.

• • •

"Honestly, Manson—it's good, clean fun. For one night, can we please stop talking about the coming racial apocalypse and simply enjoy ourselves?"

"Suit yourself, man. But don't say I didn't warn you." The auto pulled up in front of a knot of people, and Lady Unsybil fairly leapt out of the back.

"I don't like the look of this." Manson cast a baleful eye over all the knights, sparring and chaffing each other before the contest.

"If you're worried about it being violent—"

"No, it's not violent enough. They should use knives or something."

"Go park the car," Lady Unsybil said, then disappeared into a group of "ladies" wearing wimples made of stiff paper. Manson made sure she wasn't looking, then began rummaging in the glovebox. He extracted a brown glass bottle full of liquid.

"What's that?" I asked.

"Just a little something for the party." Manson saw my worried look. "Don't be such a square. It's totally natural, man. Ergot. Comes from moldy bread."

I scrambled out of the car, determined to find Lady Unsybil. I found her at the lip of a crowd, cheering madly as a young man swung a battle axe-shaped tea cozy at his opponent.

"M'lady!" I shouted. "Manson's up to something! We should go home!"

"We just got here, Percy! Go with the flow…" A wad of material tumbled through the air, thwacking a tall gent with glasses. "Ooh! A tunic cannon!"

I stood by Lady Unsybil glumly, seeing little and liking less—waist-height was good for tray-boy duties but dreadful for spectation, and I got the sense that something bad was about to happen. My illusions were not shattered when I spied Dratyew Crawly wading through the pulsing throng, brandishing a wooden sword.

"What ho!" he said. "Is this some sort of mosh-Morris Dancing?" He began a fruity-stepping sally that ended squarely on the toes of a large, rough gentleman. The gentleman did not like it, and pushing commenced; the pushes echoed throughout the crowd like ripples in a pond, and pretty soon, what had been a mellow if exuberant celebration of the Middle Ages "as they ought to have been" was teetering perilously close to a riot.

Through the tumult, I happened to spy Manson tipping something into a large container labeled "mead." Then he climbed on to a table.

"Dig! Drink this electric mead and grok what I'm laying down!" Manson shouted hoarsely into the night. "The times they are a-changing; you must get hip to the coming grooviness! Escape your ego! Follow me!" The table tipped, and the scrawny chauffeur was swallowed by a roiling tide of homemade heraldry.

I turned to Lady Unsybil. "M'lady—bad vibes—"

Before she could respond, a gaily embroidered tunic slammed into her head, knocking her to the ground.

• • •

"*That's it!*" the Earl shouted. "Manson leaves *tonight!*"

"Don't you dare!" Lady Unsybil shouted right back.

"What did she say? I couldn't quite understand it."

"I think it was, 'Don't you dare,'" Lady Marry said. "Then something about Manson trying to create his own private army."

"Can't we remove the t-shirt?" asked his lordship.

"It's dangerously embedded," Mrs. Crawly said. "Eventually it will drop off of its own accord, but to force-peel it now..."

Lady Unsybil was continuing to rant and ramble, muffled by the garment. "—I'll run away! I'll join the circus! I'll sell myself to Pancho Villa! You'll have to pay a hundred-thousand pounds, just to get me back—"

"Let's leave it," his lordship said.

"I've got an even better idea: Let's all go have a drink," Lady Cantswim whispered. "She'll never know." And snickering, they all crept out.

• • •

"Thank heaven you were there," Lady Marry said to Mr. Crawly, as they gnawed Cook's shingle-like sandwiches. "Don't forget Percy," he replied. "We loaded Lady Unsybil on his head, and the little chap carried her through like a champion. He's quite a tray-boy."

"When I left her upstairs, Unsybil was threatening to ransom herself."

"Teens love to self-dramatize."

"Indeed. The idea that Papa would pay £100,000 just to have her hippie nonsense around! Who'd ransom that?"

"Ransom?" Bits of sandwich fell from Mr. Crawly's mouth. "Blimey, I never thought of that. Here I am, sizing up the candlesticks when, right in front of me..."

"Thought of what?"

"I never realized that your father would pay money, if one of you were—I say, Marry, would you marry me?"

"Oh, Dratyew! This is so sudden. I need to think."

"We'll get married, and I'll take you on the most exotic honeymoon, say Morocco, or a cave in Mexico, or darkest Africa…Someplace beautiful, exotic, with very little policing, and no extradition treaty with Great Britain. Then I could write letters to everyone, demanding—I mean, announcing—"

"How romantic!"

"Yes, quite," Mr. Crawly said, getting up. "Now, Marry, I must go collect magazines—to cut out letters, for the announcements." Mr. Crawly slung his wooden sword through a belt-loop. "Don't make me wait too long for an answer, will you? If there's a world war, the value of the pound will sink like a stone."

•   •   •

"Hold steady now Percy," Lady Cantswim said, placing the last baseball card on the pyramid, which swayed unsteadily. Even among the rock-bottom standards of their class—a group that regularly matched wits with foxes and lost—the Cantswims brought torpor and ennui to new heights.

There was a local gust of wind, and the house blew down. "*Violent! You did it again!*"

"This isn't an official visit," the Dowager Countess said. "I just wanted to come by and say something."

"So say it. You've already ruined another morning's work."

"You did right to stand by Marry," Lady Violent said. "Otherwise there'd be no show."

"Oh, surely interesting things happen among the staff. Baits is always being discharged then coming back, and Wanna—"

Lady Violent pooh-poohed. "Yes, but who would watch that except a bunch of commoners?"

"True. Marry will be pleased to know you're back on her side."

"That I am. Only—I do wish he'd been English."

"Even if he had, it wouldn't have been English enough for you," Lady Cantswim said. "What do you always say? 'The wogs begin at East Finchley'?"

"Quite." She rummaged in her bag. "To celebrate our *rapprochement*, I have brought something from the Dower House."

Lady Cantswim regarded the green glass contraption. "A hubbly-bubbly?"

"This one was given to me in Khartoum by Chinese Gordon himself."

"Violet, how in the world did you become such a…stoner?"

"When Robber's father was in Jamaica. Serving the Empire overseas can be a difficult task, but it is not entirely a thankless one. Shall we?"

"Not me—I get terribly anxious. But you go ahead."

The old lady did so. After several big puffs, she coughed. "Did Marry use the servant's entrance?"

"She says so. How's your glaucoma?"

"Don't be impertinent. I can't imagine why I got so agitated about Marry. Who among us hasn't performed a solo on the old pink oboe?" She inhaled deeply. "We all must strike a bargain or two, to make it down the altar."

CHAPTER SEVEN.

Boom Goes La Belle Époque.
(6 July - 4 August 1914)

W hat's the point of the Season, anyway?" Lady Edict griped as the Cantswims trooped back into Downturn. They'd spent the last several months in the capital, leaving both it and themselves definitely worse for the wear.

"I can understand why it eludes you." Lady Violent was disheartened; day after day, she had watched London's eligible bachelors appraise her middle granddaughter with an enthusiasm usually reserved for gout.

"What did you say, Granny?"

"I said, 'There's always next year.'"

"Next year? God forbid. Nigel Throttlebottom practically examined my teeth."

"Let him!" Lady Cantswim said. "You inherited my strong, American teeth."

The Earl's face suddenly curdled. "Don't tell me we forgot to board the bally dog again! *Cussin!*"

"The Season's positively medieval." Lady Unsybil scratched at a henna tattoo. "Everyone hauling out the merchandise, year after year," she said glumly. "Surely there's some sort of mandatory retirement age?"

Lady Violent smiled. "I don't think you'll have to worry about that, Unsybil dear."

"Yes," Lady Edict agreed. "Them's baby-birthin' hips."

"My god, get you ladies together and the conversation goes right into the gutter." Fingers in ears, the Earl went off in search of ruined carpet. The girls went upstairs, leaving Lady Cantswim and Lady Violent.

"I'm worried about Marry," her ladyship confided. "Do you think she'll be all right, staying with Rosibuns?"

"I think she'll be fine," the Dowager Countess said. "She made quite a few friends this year, commenting on the horribleness

The Season made some women peculiarly competitive.

65

of everyone's outfits and taking bets on which side certain gentlemen 'dress' upon."

Her ladyship laughed. "Marry may die a spinster, but damn it if she's not a lot more fun. Still, it was difficult to watch. Everyone treated her like spoiled milk."

"Wait long enough, and that becomes delicious cheese."

· · ·

Downstairs, it seemed like we had never left. Cook started burning herself and dropping things, and Dhumbas and Miss O'Lyin went out for long smokes. There were two recent deaths on everyone's lips: that of the Archduke Franz Ferninand, and of Killem's mother.

"Turns out she had a whole second family in Austria," Killem said. "She was just in the wrong place at the wrong time."

"To think she was a farmer's wife and an Archduke's at the same time," Wanna said. "It's shocking."

"No shock to me," Dhumbas said, reeking of stale smoke. "Everyone's just people. It's not like the upper classes have different equipment. Upstairs, downstairs, everyone's equal behind the bushes."

Mr. Baits frowned. "If you're going to represent the new modern age, I accept that. But why must you be so grubby?"

"Grubby's the future, Mr. Baits," Dhumbas said.

"I'm afraid he's right," Mrs. Snughes said. "I just read Mr. Wells' latest: *Two Lasses, One Goblet*."

"What's it about?" Mr. Cussin asked.

"You do not wish to know."

· · ·

The next day in the library, I noticed Lord Canswim looking at me fixedly. I didn't mind. If, in the words of Lewis Carroll, "A cat may look at a King" the reverse must surely apply as well—only I wondered if I could be of help.

"M'lord? Is something the matter?"

"Your legs, Percy. Is it just me, or is there more of them? Go stand next to that statue, for scale."

I did so.

"Well, it has happened. You've grown," he sighed. "Knew we shouldn't have fed you from the kitchens. My father fed our tray-boy sawdust and clinkers, and he stayed the same height until the day he died. Which was about two weeks, but it's the principle of the thing."

"I'm sorry, m'lord, but I'm not quite following."

"Tray-boys are waist-high. As of this moment you have breached belly-button level and are steaming towards the nipple. Would you be willing to go to London for an operation?"

"An operation, m'lord?"

"Yes, to shorten you. It will be expensive, and painful, but a small price to pay to keep your job. I'll make the arrangements."

•   •   •

As I was preparing to go to London, Lady Marry was preparing to leave it. She was getting along swimmingly at Downturn House—until, that is, the afternoon her aunt Lady Rosibuns broached a sensitive subject.

"Marry," Lady Rosibuns asked as they walked in the park, "is there anything you wish to tell me?"

"Not particularly."

"Nothing having to do with romance?"

"Not much to report in that regard, I'm afraid." As she said this, however, Lady Marry's porcelain cheek belied her words; it brightened almost imperceptibly, and a trickle of sweat parted its fine down.

"My dear, you're glowing."

"It's just humid," Lady Marry said, tugging at her high collar. "Have you noticed how infrequently it rains around our family? England is as dank and gloomy as the inside of a boot, and yet the proportion of sunny days *we* must endure…"

"I have a feeling you're trying to change the subject."

"Aunt Rosibuns, you are to hinting what the Kaiser is to diplomacy."

"I apologize, Marry. Delicacy is not my strong suit," Lady Rosibuns admitted. "I have heard talk—just loose talk, which I'm not saying I believe—which touches on something I've been meaning to tell you for years. Something that your mother should've told you about, something that has affected the women in our family for generations."

"Oh, dear," Lady Marry said. "Sounds dreadful. What is it?"

"When we marry, Marry—how shall I say this?—my husband Mamaluke—our husbands die."

"Well, we can't possibly be faulted for that."

"Yes, but—in our most intimate moments, our husbands—we tend to kill them."

"My god!"

"You needn't be concerned, it's not a punishable offense."

"And why are you telling me this, now?"

"Because I sense that you genuinely care for Cousin Dratyew, and would not want to hasten his transit to the Beyond. Via your hoo-ha."

In this, Lady Marry's worst fears were spoken. As she did not trust her features, she pretended to swallow a bug. Lady Rosibuns pounded her on the back.

"Thank you," Lady Marry croaked, leaning against a poplar. "But even if I were afflicted in this way—which, how could we know, given that I am as pure and unsullied as a nun—"

"Heloise, perhaps."

"—even if I were so cursed, would that not be Dratyew's choice?"

Lady Rosibuns sighed, "I think you will find the judgment of the male quite unreliable in this regard. Once the clothes come off, the brain shuts down."

"Well," Lady Marry said, regaining herself, "I shall keep it in mind. May we turn back, Aunt Rosibuns?"

"Of course we can, dear." The demi-spinster paused and asked her neice, "Now do you see why they call me Rosibuns?"

"I'm feeling a bit slow today, I'm afraid."

"Because when you cannot eat the main course, you get awfully interested in appetizers."

"I'm not sure I follow you."

Lady Rosibuns smiled knowingly. "I'm not sure you don't."

•　•　•

The rabbit landed on my tray with an immobile thump.

"No mistake, I'm afraid," Dr. Clarkson said. "You're pregnant. And on that bombshell, here's my bill."

It fluttered to the floor; the Earl was gobsmacked. "But...how did this happen?"

"One of the footmen sneaked in at night with a turkey baster," Lady Cantswim said impatiently. "How do you *think* it happened?" Behind her Miss O'Lyin circulated, emanating ill-intent.

His lordship stood, brows knit, cogitating. "Doctor, is it possible that the child was sired by a fairy?"

"Oh, Robber, honestly. There are limits to your obsession."

"Euphemistically?" Dr. Clarkson scratched his big curl-headed noggin, unsure of what to say and unwilling to ask for clarification. "I suppose it does happen. I just delivered a child for the Duke of Crowbar."

"Well, there you go," the Earl said. "Him, siring a baby! That blighter's as 'men only' as Boodle's."

There was a small choke in the vicinity of Miss O'Lyin. Seeing her lady's maid head for the door, Cola spoke up. "O'Lyin, where are you going?"

"To spread the happy news." But Miss O'Lyin didn't look happy. She looked like she'd just kicked the Blarney Stone.

The Earl touched his wife's shoulder. "Let her tell. Fairy or not, this house is due for some good news."

"Very well. You go too, Percy. And take the rabbit. Waste not, want not."

• • •

"You bastard!" Miss O'Lyin snapped at Dhumbas. The twin jets of smoke coming out of her nostrils made her look like a bull in full rut. But it was Dhumbas' mating habits that were in question at the moment.

"Look, you know me, all right?"

"'Everyone's equal behind the bushes,' you said. Little did I know. Pervert."

"Invert, thank you very much," Dhumbas said. "Maybe it was Percy."

I froze.

"No," Miss O'Lyin fumed. "The doctor definitely said it was one of your lot. His lordship asked him, straight-out, and Clarkson said you did it 'optimistically.' He even mentioned your BFF the Duke."

"This is crazy. There is not enough lager in the universe to—"

"Of course that's what you *say*. You wouldn't be the first footman to overstep. Lying, cheating, bearing false witness…I don't even mind a little petty thievery, in its place," Miss O'Lyin said. "But rising above your station, I will not tolerate."

"I do believe the lady's jealous, don't you Percy?"

Miss O'Lyin whipped the cigarette out of Dhumbas' mouth, then ground the bright orange tip against her own forehead without the slightest change of expression. "From now on, you and I are enemies."

"Suit yourself."

"I will."

"I'm glad."

"Not as glad as I am."

"Best of luck, then."

"And you."

"I can't seem to end this scene."

"Me either."

"Just leave."

"Oh! Right."

And without another word, Miss O'Lyin turned and walked back inside.

• • •

Miss O'Lyin wasn't the only one less than pleased by the happy news. The day before Wanna and I went to London for my operation, I accompanied Cousin Dratyew and Lady Marry around the gardens with a bowl of nuts on my head. The one-time heir to Downturn was so angry, he didn't even need a nutcracker.

"Doesn't that hurt?"

"I wish it were that baby's skull! *UGGN!*"

Lady Marry put her hand on his flexing arm. "Dratyew, it might not be a boy. It could just be…a hard-boiled egg, or something."

"Crikey, Cousin Marry. You really don't know anything about sex, do you?"

"How could I?" Marry laughed ruefully. "All Mama did was call our governess into the drawing room: 'Take them to the zoo. They'll figure it out.'" The aristo-vamp twirled her parasol. "That's where Edict's horrid farm obsession took root, if you ask me. Always lurking around the chickens and sheep, trying to catch them in personal moments. Still, it's not as bad as Unsybil. She always headed straight for the reptile house, so Heaven knows what she thinks goes on. I did all right, considering," Lady Marry said. "I liked the monkeys."

"Getting back to the subject of our marriage—"

"What is your position on poo-throwing?"

"God! I haven't a clue!"

"Or picking nits? Between consenting adults, of course."

"Are you going to talk sensibly, or not?"

"Monkeys are unfairly maligned, I feel."

Mr. Crawly sighed. "I see I'm going to have to humor you."

"A friend of mine once shared the most fascinating fact about the common chimpanzee."

"Really."

"Yes. It uses the same orifice for elimination and exquisite pleasure."[3]

His face an interesting shade of reddish-purple, Mr. Crawly knocked the bowl of nuts off my tray, scattering them all over the lawn. Then he stormed off, muttering.

---

[3] Mr. Galoot was mistaken about this, as I later discovered to my profound personal reget.

• • •

"Go on, Craisy," Killem whispered. "Touch it."

"Don't make me," Craisy said. "It looks too strange."

Killem and Craisy had sneaked into Mr. Cussin's office, where the new telephone had been installed. On the desk it stood, as alien and charged with magic as an ancient Pharoah's scepter.

"No need to be frightened. I'll show you." Smiling mischievously, Killem took the little black speaking part off its perch, put it up to his bottom, and farted into it.

A tinny voice startled them both: "Hello? What was that you said?"

Laughing fit to burst, the pair tumbled out of the office in a rush—and into the arms of Mr. Cussin himself.

"And what were you two doing in my office?"

Craisy curtsied so hard she pulled a muscle.

"The telephone rang," Killem lied.

"A likely story. The telephone is not a toy. It is a useful tool, and I'll thank you to treat it as such in future."

After they were gone, the butler went into his sanctum. There, on the desk, a tinny voice was still questioning the aether: "Hello?...Would you like to place a call?"

Mr. Cussin put his hand on it, to return it to its cradle—then was seized by the most peculiar idea. He spoke into the tube.

"Hello?"

"Can I help you?" a woman's voice responded.

"Erm, yes..." Mr. Cussin slid behind his desk. "Might I ask what you are wearing?"

"Whatever for?"

"Just humor me, madam. I'm conducting an experiment."

"Well, if it's for Science...I'm wearing a housecoat."

A TELE-INAMORATA.

"Just a housecoat?"

"No, certainly! A blouse, too."

"How's it cut? Does it have buttons down the front?"

"Yes. Five or six…"

"And can you undo them?"

"Are you sure this is for Science?" The woman on the phone felt strange stirrings of her own.

"Indubitably. What else?"

"A skirt, a hoop skirt. A bustle…A petticoat. Another petticoat…A corset…"

"What kind of corset? Is it sweaty?"

"Whalebone. And very damp."

"Oh, mama—" Mr. Cussin breathed.

For the sake of decorum, we shall leave the pioneers to their discoveries.

•   •   •

"You know, Cousin Dratyew," Lord Cantswim said, as Whatsit trotted beside, "if it's a boy and you're chucked out, I'll make whatever provisions I can."

"'Provisions'? What does that mean, exactly?"

"Look!" Lord Cantswim leaned over to pluck something from the turf. "A fairy beret! Now *these* are rare."

"Acorn top."

"Really. And I suppose you'll tell me these aren't fairy snowshoes?"

"Maple seeds. Lord Cantswim, don't change the subject," Mr. Crawly said crossly. "What possible provision could you make?"

"Well, I could…I'll give you some coupons for Speedball."

Mr. Crawly kept silent and let the Earl squirm. He'd had enough Cantswim eccentricity for several lifetimes.

"I mean, it's not good to stick with," his lordship said, "but it can distract one." Much to the Earl's relief, Lady Edict shouted from an upstairs window of the Abbey. "Papa! Send Percy up—I need to post some letters."

I didn't say anything, but the Earl must've seen the fear on my face; his middle daughter wrote in bulk. "Go on, lad. You'll get your reward in Heaven."

"At least somebody's getting some reward," Mr. Crawly grumbled.

•   •   •

True to form, Lady Edict had loaded me down like a pack animal—whereas she herself carried nothing but gloves. (The day was, as usual, sunny.)

"Come on, tray-boy, do try to keep up."

As we rounded a corner near the top of the stairs, a slim arm grabbed Lady Edict; she turned suddenly to see Lady Marry in high color. "Did you tell?"

"Marry, do you know that your face looks rather like a kabuki mask at the moment?"

"Sod kabuki! Did you write a nasty letter about me and Mr. Galoot?"

Lady Edict said nothing.

"Don't deny it," Lady Marry pressed further. "Evelyn Staplier told me he saw it in *Naughty Ladies Magazine*. He only reads it for the articles."

"With a name like Evelyn, I can believe it," Lady Edict sniffed, disengaging her arm. "Come, tray-boy. I shouldn't get too close to Lady Marry's baby bits if I were you. They kill."

• • •

The next morning, breakfast service was more fun than usual—for me, at least. Lady Edict and Lady Marry sat opposite each other, glaring. Each sister had a small doll and was poking hatpins into it. One would poke, and the other would writhe, or gasp, or give a stifled scream. When Lady Edict clutched her bowels and skittered from the room, his lordship turned to me. "You may go, Percy. You mustn't miss your train to London."

"After what we paid?" her ladyship said. "If you miss it, kid, I'll go down there and have the operation myself." By her expression it was clear that the lady of the house thought her husband was being too soft-hearted and spendthrift, so I ran out of there before she changed his mind.

London! What an adventure! And I got to go with Wanna, who was mousy-hot, and thus not as scary to ten-year-old me.

As she and I hurried downstairs, we got a glimpse inside Lady Cantswim's chambers. Coated in woodchips and plaster dust, Miss O'Lyin was unrolling an Oriental rug over a large hole in the floor.

"What are you doing, Miss O'Lyin?"

"If I were you, I'd spend less time worrying about the affairs of others, and more time avoiding the thin wire strung across the hall at ankle-level."

Wanna leaned down, and plucked the wire with her finger. Instantly darts shot from hidden ports in either wall, embedding themselves into the woodwork with a thunk. "Curare-tipped?"

"Of course," Miss O'Lyin said. "Boy! Mind the bear trap!"

I stepped briskly to the side; a few more inches and my shortening trip would've been quite unnecessary.

"Don't sit in judgment on me," the lady's maid demanded. "I have my reasons."

"You always do," Wanna said. "Just wondering, does insanity run in your family?"

"I shouldn't like to say; does nosiness run in yours?"

With trouble obviously brewing, I was glad to get away from Downturn Abbey for a while. And I was gladder still after what Wanna told me on the train. Twenty miles outside Bumbleford, she pulled down my copy of *Lo! A Journal of What Will Be.*

"Hey! I'm reading that!"

"Percy, you're not going to have any operation. It's barbaric."

"If you say so."

"I do say so. It's not even a proper hospital. It's a veterinary clinic," Wanna said. "I've already fixed everything with Mr. Baits. He's going to put lifts in all his lordship's shoes, and you and I are going to take this money, and do up the town."

• • •

The trip was, I'm afraid, a bit of a let down. I was glad to avoid the operation, that much is true, but "doing up London" actually consisted of accompanying Wanna all over the city digging up facts about Mr. Baits. According to *Lo!*, someday one will be able to sit at one's desk and find out all manner of things, using some sort of electric-powered "computation engine." I don't quite understand the details, but if *Lo!* says it, that's good enough for me.

Getting back to Mr. Baits: It seemed he'd been married years ago, and had taken the rap for a wife of dubious character. No one could say why he'd done it, but that was typical for Mr. Baits. In addition to a mysterious past and a thing for privacy, he also had a mother who smelled like Caffey's Rhubarb Liniment.

"Genghis was her name," Mrs. Baits said. "Genghis Hitler. A mean woman, greedy, too, and full of bad ideas. Somehow she'd got it into her head that she could steal Balmoral Castle."

"I sense this story won't end well," I said.

"It did not. When they caught her, all Genghis said was, 'I couldn't find a big enough sack.'"

Wanna nibbled a biscuit. "So she had poor spatial judgment, as well."

"Has."

"Sorry?"

"You said 'had,'" Mrs. Baits corrected. "To my knowledge, Genghis Hitler is still among the living."

"*Ree-ally.*" Wanna opened her purse and checked for her heavy cosh. "Do you happen to know where she lives?"

"No, I don't."

The purse snapped shut. "Oh well, all in good time. But why would your son confess to a crime that his wife had committed?"

Mrs. Baits had a twinkly smile just like her son. "Not very familiar with romantic heroes, are you?"

"Are you kidding? The only romance I've had in the last five years involved sneaking a jar of leaky solvents into his lordship's desk, then serving elevenses in a homemade Tinkerbell costume."

"Dating's hard," Mrs. Baits clucked sympathetically. "Confessing, that was just his nature. My Jon was always like that, even as a boy. He confessed to starting the Black Death, bumping the Leaning Tower of Pisa—mind you, we'd never gone to Italy. We'd never been further abroad than the Isle of Dogs. I still remember the day he learned about the Crucifixion." Mrs. Baits grew misty-eyed. "Mustn't have been more than seven. 'I did it, Mummy,' he said, all puffed up and straight, like a little man. 'I killed our Lord and Savior.'

"Forgive a mother's tears. The confessing seemed like just a habit. I felt sure he'd grow out of it. Never dreamed it'd get him into so much trouble." She glanced out the window. "Rain's started again. If Jon were here, he'd confess to that, too."

• • •

When Wanna and I returned home, the Abbey's mood was deep black.

Following a £5 note on a fishing line, Lady Cantswim had stepped out of the bath, slipped on a greased corridor, careened down a hall only inches ahead of a huge boulder, fell against a bust of Shakespeare which tipped and activated a trapdoor, dropped through a passage lined with daguerreotypes of Dhumbas with the eyes scratched out, and finally landed in a Burmese tiger trap.

No fetus, not even one of noble blood, could survive that. "And it was a boy..." the Earl said sadly.

"...Either that, or Italian food," Dhumbas said downstairs. "Dr. Clarkson didn't let me get a proper look."

The rest of the staff gasped. Mr. Baits shot to his feet and grabbed the first footman by the neck.

"Is this meant to frighten me, Mr. Baits?" Dhumbas whispered. "Because it isn't. However, if you're trying to turn me on..."

"Let him go!" Mr. Cussin's eyes flashed fire. "Just for that, Dhumbas, you will be the Guest of Honor at this year's summer party! Any objections?"

"I think that's a grand idea," Miss O'Lyin said.

Dhumbas registered surprise; as of twelve hours ago, they'd been sworn enemies. "You're a queer one."

"That's rich, coming from you."

"I'm reappropriating the word. Ask Lady Unsybil; she'll explain the concept."

Killem spoke up. "I thought the party would be cancelled, on account of the baby. Well, *ex*-baby."

"On the contrary," Mrs. Snughes said. "Not with such a deserving Guest of Honor. And now is precisely when some good cheer is necessary."

"There will be no cancellation," Mr. Cussin rumbled. "No traditions are more sacred to the upperclasses than those involving free food."

"Guest of Honor, that's more like it." Dhumbas said, straightening his shirt and jacket. "What goodies does it entail?"

Mrs. Snughes smiled. "Now, now, Dhumbas. You know the ladies arrange this affair."

"You'll find out soon enough," Wanna added. She and Gwon were smirking, and the look on Miss O'Lyin's face was...how I imagine Satan looks when a priest bangs his finger, I'll leave it at that.

"Will I get extra pay?"

"Of course!" Mr. Cussin said. "Only—I'll give it to you after."

• • •

Every August, the people around Downturn Abbey gathered together, in woods and fields, sheltered copses and woodsy hollows sacred from before the time of the Romans, to thank the spirits and the Good Mother Earth for the bounty she'd provided. As befit the age, humble people gathered in humble places, townsfolk gathered with townsfolk, and the area's gentry gathered on the lawn of Downturn.

As his lordship was obliged to provide plenty of food and drink, her ladyship disapproved virulently. She surveyed the grazing gentry with a sour expression.

"Robber, I do not understand why we have to lay out a fortune just because of some pagan superstition! The finger food alone...Not to mention that wicker man. It's horrible. Can't we at least make it out of metal, and re-use it?"

"Then it wouldn't burn, my dear," the Earl said evenly. "I wouldn't expect an American to understand it. It is an old tradition, and sometimes it's wise to honor the old ways."

Downturn's butler cleared his throat. "Speaking of, m'lord, Mrs. Snughes tells me that the Dhumbas portion of today's festivities has gone without a hitch."

"Good. How do they knock him out, Cussin?"

"Some draught that Cook makes, m'lord. I've tried to get it out of her many a time, but she's firm. Says it's an old family recipe."

"Remind me never to get on her bad side," his lordship chuckled. "Cola, do you need anything before Cussin disappears into the milling crowd?"

"No," she said. After Mr. Cussin had left, she said to Lord Cantswim, "Maybe we'll make a profit on the day anyway."

"I keep telling you, I will not sell tickets to the bonfire."

"It's Sir Antony Strangler. I think he's going to propose to Edict."

"Splendid! We'll let the happy couple light the leg."

• • •

"Lady Marry," Sir Antony asked, "do you know where I can find your sister?"

"Unsybil, or Edict? If it's the latter, do prepare to have your ear chewed off."

"THAT'S SO HOT. I mean, why?"

"She's terribly proud of herself. Apparently the local constabulary wants her help catching a mysterious psychopath."

"How unfortunate."

"Not to hear Edict tell it—she's pleased as punch. She's even wearing a wire... Why Sir Antony, where are you going?"

Lady Marry fiddled with her brastrap as we looked at the cloud of dust. "Odd man, Percy, don't you think?"

I did not have time to respond— Lady Edict walked over, a startled look on her face. "I say, where's Sir Antony's sprinting off to? Did some wag tell him he was the guest of honor?"

Lady Marry locked eyes with her sister. Then she licked her thumb and pressed it against the empty air.

To further the illusion, Lady Marry had hired a car and stenciled it thusly.

"*Ssssst!*" she hissed. "Burned you! Mess with the best, die like the rest."

Lady Edict started to say something…then just floated away, lip trembling. Even after all that she'd done, I felt quite bad for her. It wasn't her fault she was a secondary character.

•   •   •

Unfortunately by the end of the party, Lady Marry was no happier than her sister. I was standing next to his lordship when Mr. Crawly rushed up, quite perturbed.

"Ah, Cousin Dratyew. Are you enjoying yourself?"

"Not much I'm afraid. Your daughter has declined to marry me."

"But why?" the Earl asked, genuinely pained.

"She would not say. Or, at least, nothing she said made the least bit of sense. Muttered something about 'the stripey hole' and not wanting to be made a double-murderess."

"Well, perhaps you will consider it a lucky escape," the Earl said, patting Mr. Crawly on the shoulder. "All the women in my family are crazy."

"Thank goodness we men are made of sterner stuff."

"Indeed," the Earl said. "I do hope the Fairy King finally comes today, don't you? Every year, I stick an invitation in the big willow, and I must say I'm beginning to feel a bit hurt."

•   •   •

Dhumbas "came to" around five in the afternoon, so the last portion of the party was garlanded by the usual accompaniment of plaints, issuing from the head of the structure at the bottom of the lawn. As the rest of us had predicted, Dhumbas was both more profane, and more self-pitying, than the usual sacrifice.

"You bastards! You tricked me!" he said, beating against the slats. "You're doing this because I'm different!"

"No, we're not!" Wanna hollered. "It's because you're an arsehole!" (She had consumed several shandies, in case you couldn't tell.)

"Percy, you have to help me! Craisy! When it comes time to light it, don't!"

"Sorry, Dhumbas," Craisy said. "For me, this is like Christmas."

Smiling, Mr. Baits looked at his pocket watch. "Not long now, Dhumbas."

"Aye," Mrs. Snughes said, "and it couldn't happen to a nicer chap!"

"By which she means 'bloody great git'!" Gwon shouted. (Shandies.)

"But Gwon! You represent changing social mores! That's me! I'm all for that!"

"Oh give it a rest," Wanna said. "Appeasing the gods is the one useful thing you'll do with your life."

As we were all standing at the base of the great wicker figure, making bets on how long it would take this year, Killem ran up, red-faced and out of breath. "Take this—it's for his lordship! As quick as you can!" He slapped a small envelope on my tray, and I sped up the length of the lawn as fast as my short legs could carry me.

The Earl was sitting next to his wife. "Darling, I am sure that fairies do not carry the French Pox."

Mr. Cussin leaned over and whispered something in his lordship's ear. "That is regrettable," the Earl said, "but I'm not sure 'declining standards' has anything to do with it."

I pushed in. "Telegram for you, m'lord," I panted.

The Earl slit it open, and we all watched the blood drain from his face as he read its contents. Without a word, he stood up and walked to the center of the lawn.

"My lords, ladies and gentlemen!" he announced. "I regret to inform you that we are in for a spot of unpleasantness with Germany."

"Tell us something we haven't been preparing for!" someone shouted.

"Also—Mr. Cussin informs me that we are out of sherry."

The effect of this news on the crowd was galvanic; they streamed away in every direction, to enlist, consume more drink, or both. "End of a bally era," I heard someone mumble. "'Spect it will rain buckets tomorrow," another said.

There was no more thought of celebration, not that day. Though we were all too heartbroken to assist, eventually Dhumbas broke out of the wicker man and let himself down, heading for parts unknown.

What happened that day—the outbreak of War—certainly saved Dhumbas' life. And I bet he didn't even thank Mrs. Snughes.

END OF PART ONE.

CHAPTER EIGHT.

War is...Unpleasant
(1916)

At 12, my growth, like the clash of armies all around the world, could not be stopped. Though this would've meant the end of my time in service during the pre-War days, the manpower shortage allowed me to stay on at Downturn. Only not as tray-boy; that grew more absurd by the inch. I was now a thing-boy.

The position is unknown today, and was rare even then; only the poshest households employed a thing-boy but, vanity aside, I believe I was very useful indeed. A thing-boy walked around the house wearing a puffy, smock-ish sort of garment lined with pockets, inside each of which was a useful household item. Postage stamps, mucilage, a gun.

This last came in handy when I was sent abroad to assist Mr. Crawly. Downturn's heir had enlisted in the Second Yorkshire Light Infantry, nicknamed "The King's Own Poseurs," thinking that a high preponderance of artistic types would make the unit less useful when it came to combat. Unfortunately, the utter lack of creative talent shown by members of the regiment, as well as their unerring instinct to practice their hobbies in the most irritating ways possible, actually made HQ more likely to send them into battle. "The attack failed to reach any objective, but at least we thinned out the Poseurs."

The blatantly sacrificial nature of the unit wasn't the only bit of bad news waiting for me in France. Newspaper reports to the contrary, a soldier's life wasn't all rum and grateful Belgian women. One did get plenty of fresh air, and meet some interesting people, but on the whole, I could've skipped it. Bad food and worse weather, horrid smells and disease, and of course the ever-present spectre of sudden death—one had to become insensible to these, just to survive.

Lieutenant Crawly, a true Cantswim and thus insensible to most everything, thrived.

"Percy, what's another way to say 'snuffed it'?" he shouted as shells fell and bullets sang all around us.

"Can't think now, sir!" I screamed into the dirt wall of the trench.

"Bloody lot of help you are..."

I opened my mouth to speak, and some dirt flew into it. Before I could clear my airway, the sergeant-major blew his whistle: time for the attack.

Lieutenant Crawly's eyes lit up. "Been wanting to do this the entire war!"

Retrieving a football from I know not where, Lieutenant Crawly gleefully tossed it over the parapet. It did not even touch ground before being torn to pieces by Hunnish machine-gun fire. The men gawped at the ruined shreds, visualizing their own innards.

"Obviously defective!" Lieutenant Crawly shouted, and mounted the fire-step. "Poseurs, forward!"

The sight is burned into my mind as if it were yesterday: all those young men—admittedly not the flower of the Empire, they were much too annoying, but certainly taxpayers—all clambering over the top to certain doom. They stayed in formation, just as they were taught, looking hither and yon for evocative imagery, occasionally referring to a pocket thesaurus. If they'd shot back, or even dodged, they might've had a chance; but no, these were War Poets, each searching for that single bit of metered prose that would win the war for Britain.

Lieutenant Crawly and I struck boldly forward. Him a bit more boldly than I, given that I was weighted down with a smock full of flares, wire-cutters, spare goloshes, Timothy White's Sun Cream, a chaise-lounge in the event of more leisurely fighting, et cetera. Not that I was complaining, mind you; more than one time, the plethora of junk I was hauling deflected a German bullet aimed for my heart. Still, the King's Own Poseurs lost 75% in that first few minutes, and doubtless Lieutenant Crawly and I would've been among them had a stray piece of shrapnel not shattered m'lord's nib.

"Won't save you, Jerry! I have not yet begun to write!" Lieutenant Crawly turned left, where I was cowering in a shell-hole. "Give us a spare, thing-boy."

"That was the spare, Lieutenant."

"Damn! Damn and blast! I've got a bit of imagery that'll blow this war wide open. It's deucedly—deucedly—"

"Ironic?"

"Yes! That!"

"Well, don't worry, sir, it will pass."

"Oh, I shouldn't think so, Percy. It's much too—"

"Sir? You might want to duck?"

"I've been thinking about it since I was in the dugout. It's about—damn it. It's totally slipped my mind."

"Well, sir"—a bullet hit the edge of my helmet, knocking it crooked— "perhaps if we went back to the dugout, it would come back to you."

The Lieutenant considered, his hair ruffled by a murderous German traverse. "I suppose you're right."

As we crawled back towards safety, Lieutenant Crawly cast a backward glance at the rest of his company, scrambling now, composing in twos and threes, being torn to ribbons. Scraps of foolscap and pages from rhyming dictionaries were falling like snow. It would be another long night, I thought, listening to the Poseurs injured or caught on the wire, declaiming, until a sniper put them out of their misery. Usually it was a German sniper, but sometimes (it was said) our side couldn't help themselves. Everyone's a critic.

When we got back to the dugout, salvation was waiting for us. Lieutenant Crawly's leave had come through. I went with him.

• • •

Life back at Downturn Abbey seemed utterly unreal. There had been so many changes—Dhumbas was gone, Lady Unsybil had decided to help the war effort by becoming a clock—and yet it was forever the same, forever Downturn.

That is not to say that the manor didn't contain its share of dangers. The night Cousin Dratyew introduced his new fiancé to the family—well, let's just say that it made France seem friendly. It was at a musical performance to raise money for the troops; a band of musicians from Ripping were engaged and, while the music wasn't exactly to my taste, it did seem to fit that discordant evening quite precisely.

As the guests took their seats in the great hall, Lieutenant Crawly ambled up to Lord and Lady Cantswim. His new girl, a pleasant enough strawberry blonde, looked terrified. I felt something hot on the back of my neck, then turned and saw Lady Marry glaring from across the room.

"Lady Cantswim, may I introduce my fiancée, Miss Lineolia Swiffer."

"HA!" Lady Marry barked, for no reason at all.

Her ladyship tried to ignore her. "What a lovely name."

"HA!"

"Killem, would you go anesthetize my daughter? You'll find the hypodermic in the drawer of my nightstand, labeled 'Think of England'...I'm sorry, my dear, you were saying?"

"That's quite all right, Lady Cantswim. My name is the female of 'linoleum,' actually. My father made his money in flooring."

"Well, you shall tell us more at dinner," the Earl said. "They are beginning again."

> "I am he as you are he as you are me and we are all together...
> See how they run like pigs from a gun
> I'm crying."

I was seated next to Lady Violent, pulling ear trumpet duty. "Do you think by 'pigs' he means the Germans?" I heard her murmur. "But then why would he be crying?"

Suddenly, two horrid women stood up. One blonde, the other brunette, they looked to be no more than twenty. Extracting them from a secret compartment under their skirts, the pair began distributing live chickens to any young men out of uniform. The dark-haired one had just given a pullet to Killem when Lord Cantswim threw a sprocket.

Even the pair's hosery was objectionable.

"STOP THIS AT ONCE!"

"Oh, stop yourself," the blonde said boldly.

"Yeh, this man is a coward!" They both walked around poor Killem, strutting and scratching. "Bok bok bok…Bok bok bok…"

We all watched in astonishment; I have never seen a better impression. You could practically see the chickens circling our blushing footman. Finally the Earl's outrage overtopped their acting ability, and he butted in.

"Are you finished?"

"Nearly," one of the girls said, then the other gave a final ear-splitting "B'GAWK!"

"Since you are so all-fired anxious to help the war effort," the Earl declared, "I think I shall exercise one of the few remaining privileges of my title and draft you both immediately!"

In an instant, their faces changed from defiant to frightened. "But—you can't—"

"I can, and I have," his lordship said. "You are now soldiers of His Majesty's Fairy Forces fighting in France."

"But we're female!"

"You should've been content with boating," the Dowager Countess humphed.

"Shh, Mama. Now, both of you are to report to the Ripping train station at six a.m., two days hence. Pack for mud." The Earl turned. "Now Mr. Cussin, will you please eject these two?"

As they were frog-marched to the exit, the sobbing brunette turned to her equally teary companion. "It's all your fault! I wanted to go to the movies!"

• • •

"Dratyew," a heavy-lidded Lady Marry said as they supped, "I must tell you how pleased we all are on your engorgement."

"Don't you mean—"

A pointed look from Lady Marry demonstrated exactly what she meant.

"Erm…" Lieutenant Crawly grasped for conversation. "How's your father?"

"A bit down-hearted, I'm afraid. His offer to be Generalissimo of the Fairies has fallen on deaf ears. So he'll be at Downturn for the duration."

"Thank goodness."

"Why? What's it like over there? Is it terrible?"

The soldier fidgeted with his second auxiliary soup spoon. "What was your favorite song tonight? I rather liked the one about being sixty-four…"

"Dratyew, you can be frank with me," Lady Marry said. "I'm no longer the silly girl you knew. I know about life."

"Really?"

"Really. I've changed. Haven't you?"

"Oh yes," Lieutenant Crawly said. "I realize now there are things more important than money. Not, for example, getting one's arse shot off."

"And that is why we must speak truthfully to each other," Lady Marry said, "at least while I am still somewhat sedated. What is it like? Please tell me."

"You're sure?"

"Yes, I'm sure! For goodness sake, how bad could it be?"

Lieutenant Crawly had Lady Marry retching up consommé in no time.

"All right, you've proved it—please stop—'

"And then of course there are the *nasty* bits…"

Slowly, inexorably, all other conversation at the table stopped, as detail after detail spilled forth. Shrapnel-wounds…the color of intestines…trenchfoot. Caught up in his narrative, and punishing the woman who jilted him, Lieutenant Crawly only realized the size of his audience when everyone bolted from the table.

Lady Marry gasped, then clamped her hands over her mouth as her dinner wrenched loose from its moorings. Lieutenant Crawly followed her upstairs and down, filling in colorful details. "Rats prefer the eyeball, don't you know!" he shouted through the door of the upstairs water-closet. "It's full of vitamins!"

This lasted for the better part of an hour, at the end of which, a pale and sweaty Lady Marry emerged. "Lucky for me, I'll forget most of that after the hypo wears off. Percy," she said weakly, "you are never going back to France again."

"But Marry! Percy is essential to my art," Lieutenant Crawly said, totally ignoring my joyous whoops and dancing.

"Oh, sod your art. Take Killem."

Better him than me.

• • •

It was gallant for Lady Marry to wake up with the cock's crow and tread down to Ripping Station to see Lieutenant Crawly off for France. What I minded was being dragged along with her.

"Oh, stop yawning, Percy," she said. "That stuffed animal isn't heavy." The item in question was a large hippopotamus made of pink felt almost as tall and broad as I was. Keeping it out of the mud had been murder; putting up with the stench of it, even more so. It hadn't been washed since Lady Marry was a baby. "I'm keeping you at Downturn. You could at least show a little gratitude."

"I'll try, m'lady." My gaze swept the platform. Behind Lady Marry the two girls from the recital were sobbing, suitcases in hand. They'd be sent back soon enough—some brass hat would spot "Generalissimo of His Majesty's Fairies" sooner or later—but I hoped that military inefficiency would give them at least a little taste of what they'd been so anxious for others to experience.

Lieutenant Crawly walked up, grip in hand. "Cousin Marry!"

"I just had to see you off," she said quickly. "And give you this."

I handed over the large sour-smelling soft toy.

"Thank you?"

"It's a sort of good luck charm," Marry said. "I've had it since I was small."

The soldier picked some dried zwieback off its snout. "Yes, I believe you have."

• • •

None of us liked Mr. Baits' wife, not even Miss O'Lyin who, for all her faults, unerringly recognized her betters. Or, in this case, her worses. Just how much worse we did not realize, until Mrs. Snughes asked me to spy for her.

"Percy, go up into the drop ceiling and listen to what they say."

"Mrs. Snughes, are you sweet on Mr. Baits, too?"

"Of course not, cheeky boy!" Mrs. Snughes blushed; events since 1914 had made Kaiser Bill considerably less sexy. "It's just that—I feel it may be important to the plot."

She gave me a boost and up I climbed. "Don't sneeze," she said.

I crouched on the acoustic tiles in the crawlspace above their heads, trying to keep my weight on the flimsy metal grid that supported them, It wasn't easy—if my weight shifted, I'd go right through.

Genghis was really laying down the law. Why had Mr. Baits married her in the first place?

"You're going to leave this house, tonight," she said.

"And what if I say no?"

"I'm going to tell the newspapers about Lady Marry and a certain Turk."

"Since Turkey's on the German side, they'll probably give her a medal," the valet shot back. "Put a blue plaque in the upstairs bedroom. 'Here was fired the first shot of the War.' Schoolgirls will be taught about it."

"Could be," Genghis purred. "But there's another way to tell it, isn't there? First, consorting with Turks, and now I hear tell she's prowling London bookshops asking after suspicious books. 'Psychopathia Sexualis by Richard Freiherr von Kraft-Ebing'—does that sound English to you?"

My hand slipped with the shock of it, and I nearly fell through.

"What was that noise? Above us?"

"Mice, probably. Genghis, your lies prove nothing. Latined-up smut has been an upper-class prerogative for centuries. The top shelf of the Earl's library—"

"And how would you know about that, Baitsy? Miss Snogg not living up to her name? Oh, I forgot," she said, oozing false sympathy, "you're trapped…"

With great effort, Mr. Baits kept his temper. "Is that all you've got to say?"

"No. I'd—" They both looked up at the ceiling as the tile cracked ominously. Sweat rolled down my face as I tried to will myself lighter.

"—think people this loaded could afford an exterminator…Tell you what I'll do," Genghis said, smoothing her toothbrush moustache. "Just to give us a fresh start, I'll throw in the key to that little contraption hiding in your britches." She poked Mr. Baits' groin, and he gave a jump of pain.

"You b—" Mr. Baits' response was cut short by my falling through. The small table between them was smashed to kindling, and for a moment all three of us were sprawled amidst the ruins.

"Sorry," I said, scrambling to my feet.

Genghis' face was Mephistophelian. "Rats, eh? You know what I do with rats!" Malevolence-in-a-petticoat advanced upon me, and before I could escape, a pair of strong hands had grabbed my noggin and was forcing it towards her mouth. I believe the bloody lunatic was trying to eat me.

Luckily, Mr. Baits was on her like a flash. "No, Genghis, no! The spatial judgment! He's too big!"

"NOM-NOM-NOM!" It took a moment for Mr. Baits to pull her off; luckily for me, all his worse half could manage was a few ragged mouthfuls of hair. I scrambled out into the servants' hall at the first opportunity, and rested there, chest heaving, heart pounding, knowing just how close I'd come to snuffing it.

"What's the matter with you?" Miss O'Lyin said. "You call that a haircut?"

"Eat me," I said, and stumbled away.

CHAPTER NINE.

There Once Was a Man in Ypres Salient...
(April 1917)

After Lady Unsybil enrolled in the Women's Ladies Auxiliary Defence Timekeeping Corps Brigade, usefulness spread through Downturn like ringworm. Killem enlisted, and even Lady Edict put down her poison pen long enough to help a local farmer. Everyone was so relieved at the cessation of corrosive epistolary that they overlooked her loam-stained underthings—except Lady Marry, of course. She couldn't resist a few cracks about her younger sister "finally getting her furrow plowed."

The one great exception to this trend was Bang!, Downturn's hasty hire following Mr. Baits' decampment. He seemed queerly distracted...almost as if he'd spent the previous two years in constant fear of being shot, stabbed, gassed, blown up, set on fire—or being executed for being afraid of being shot, stabbed, gassed, *et cetera*.

"BANG!" the Earl shouted, causing the man to jump a country mile. "When I asked you to dress me in my uniform, I meant military togs, not a French maid's uniform!"

"Please don't shout my name," the poor sod said, adjusting his feet to hide the puddle.

"Then don't bollocks everything up!" His lordship slapped Bang!'s hand away crossly. "I'll unhook my own stockings, thank you very much. I'm not entirely useless, no matter what the Army says." The Earl looked pensively at the garter in his hand. "God, how I wish I were in France."

•   •   •

Meanwhile, back in France, Dratyew Crawly was ensconced in his sloppy dugout, hard at work on his latest masterpiece. He'd recently fastened on the limerick form as his unique way to achieve artistic immortality.

"Listen to this," he said to the runner unlucky enough to be standing there.

"If I do, will you take this order so I can leave?"

"Maybe." Lieutenant Crawly cleared his throat.

"There once was a man on Ypres salient,
Whose male equipment was quite gaily bent.
This corkscrew arrangement

Caused his lovers derangement
Because whenever he came, up he went."

"I don't get it," the orderly said.

"You know, like a jet of water." Lieutenant Crawly twirled his finger. "And I suppose you could do better?"

"Perhaps another form, sir. A noncom in the next sector is doing wonderful things in haiku." He closed his eyes.

'*Half-man, half-carrot*
Stuck eye-deep in Flanders dirt
Cheers, Farmer Death.'

Went down spiffing at the last regimental slam. Perhaps you could do villanelle, or sestina?"

Lieutenant Crawly scowled. "Or perhaps you should give me the bloody message and get out, you Philistine." He grabbed the message and slit it open. His face fell—he was going home.

"Bet Sassoon's behind this," he muttered darkly. "Him, or Graves. They're afraid of me. Afraid of my talent."

"I'm sure that's it, sir."

"Are you chaffing me, Private? Because if you are, poet or no poet, I'll give you the kind of pranging—"

Just then, a new barrage commenced. Because, you know, all the others had been so successful.

• • •

I stood at the side of her ladyship, as Miss O'Lyin did her hair. "It's not cheap, but a thing-boy is useful, isn't it, O'Lyin?"

"Whatever you say, m'lady."

"O'Lyin, with the War on, I can't help but feel Downturn is changing."

"How do you mean, m'lady?"

"I feel there's a lower level of meaningless conniving. Would you agree?"

"I would, m'lady."

"I'm bored. You know what always gets me out of a funk? Making really terrible judgments on whom to trust," her ladyship said. "Tell me, who does the staff hate most?"

"Speaking of Dhumbas, m'lady, I just got a letter. He's been wounded."

"How did it happen?" Lady Cantswim gasped. "Will he survive?"

"Yes, thank heaven. It seems to have been some sort of prank."

89

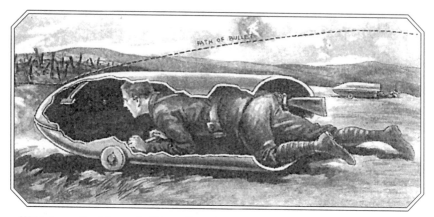

Within hours of arriving on the Western Front, Dhumbas had attempted to crawl to Switzerland. Unforutnately, before he set off, some wag turned him towards the German lines.

"Honestly, O'Lyin, what is it about men? They're in the middle of a war, for God's sake. You'd think they could be serious."

"I know, m'lady," Miss O'Lyin said. "It's not right. People pick on Dhumbas because he's so sensitive. But he says he'd like to come back to Downturn Abbey, if he's welcome."

"Make it happen, O'Lyin. Make it happen."

• • •

And speaking of poor decisions, not everyone was concentrating on the War at hand. Take the younger Mr. Marley, for example. With only Mrs. Crawly rattling around in the Crawly House, he had time to attend to other matters. Unfortunately for him, he fastened on Wanna Snogg who, after Mr. Baits' mysterious departure, could rightly be sued for false advertising.

"Did you get the book I left for you?"

"I did." It was a cheery little tome called *Love The One You're With*, quite popular at the time, and useful, too. "But then Ethyl vomited on it, I'm afraid."

"I see." Ethyl was Gwon's replacement, who drank so much you could light her sweat. This made her popular with Craisy, and no one else. "So...do you think we could ever, y'know..."

"I don't think that's going to happen," Wanna said.

"All right."

"It's like, if you were a woman, and you had a child, and that child was shot to the Moon, would you ever stop thinking about it?"

"Perhaps in the daytime."

"Or if that child was a knife, would you ever stop asking people to stab you, right in the heart, just on the off-chance that knife was him?"

"Okay, I get it."

"Or if that child were turned into a special tingly ointment, would you ever stop rubbing—"

"Fine! Fine!"

"Or if—

Halfway out the door, Mr. Marley hollered over his shoulder, "It's called therapy, Wanna. *Christ*."

•   •   •

After dinner, the Crawly clan was scattered around the drawing room like so much exquisitely tailored shrapnel. Chatting was general and, apart from the womb-freezing looks directed in Lineolia's direction, gay enough.

The Earl and Captain Crawly stood in a corner sucking on cigars. Lady Marry watched them intently from afar, drawing all sorts of conclusions from her new reading.

"So you'll be safe for a bit?" his lordship asked. "And a Captain?"

"Yes, I'm attached to General Nutt."

"Ah yes," the Earl said, "the hero of Futilité Ridge."

"*Second* Futilité," the soldier corrected. "Or Third. Or Fourth? They all blur."

"I only know schoolboy French, Cousin Dratyew, but it's almost as if God is trying to send us a message…Is old Nutt as odd as everyone says?"

"Indeed," Captain Crawly said. "He spent lots of time in the Orient."

"Changes a man."

"The funny thing is, Cousin Robber, that's the secret to his success. He doesn't fight the Germans, he just lets them advance. Then, when they get tired and distracted and full of women and drink, he simply walks in behind, cuts their lines of communication, and takes them prisoner. Ten thousand Jerries captured without a shot."

"Remarkable."

"'These are my rules,' the General said to me, 'One, pursue the opponent relentlessly and defeat him. Two, success may require complete surrender. And three, the real opponent is always oneself.'"

"How strange." Lord Cantswim relit his cigar. "Still, we take victories, no matter how they come. Cousin Dratyew, I'm wondering if you might be able to help with something. Mrs. Phatore's nephew has gone missing, and I'm trying to find out what happened to him, the poor chap."

"I expect they pre-killed him," Captain said, craning his neck slightly to the left. He enjoyed this vantage point immensely, because it allowed him to have impure thoughts about both Lady Marry and Lineolia at the same time.

"*Pre*-killed? What do you mean, pre-killed?"

"It's a new programme. The War Office figures they're going to die anyway, so why not snuff a certain percentage 'in-house,' as it were? Frightfully efficient; cheaper, too…The Boche are doing the same thing. It's a gentlemen's agreement."

"Suddenly the war makes so much more sense," his lordship said. "I used to think, 'They wouldn't just keep fighting with no result, that's preposterous. There has to be some end game, some meaning to the slaughter.'"

Captain Crawly smiled without humor. "If only, Cousin Robber. All of us are lonely ciphers wandering through a wilderness of horror and absurdity, en route to a meaningless death. That is our modern age. And also, wristwatches."

The Earl ground cigar ash into the carpet. "And people wonder why I believe in fairies," he grumbled.

• • •

"Hello!" Lady Edict trilled, as I loped behind.

The Fakes slinked out of their dilapidated farm house. This was the only structure I ever saw hang at a more precarious angle than the North Gallery of Downturn. When Mr. Fake shut the front door, the back half of the roof defiantly settled to the ground.

I recognized the couple from Chapter Two, and from Mrs. Fake's pinched, angry expression, I wagered it was probably time for a checkup. Not knowing who we were or why we'd come, only that we'd had a bath since 1915, poor Mrs. Fake adopted the typical stance of the powerless: deny everything. "If this is about the dead dog in the well, we don't know owt."

"No, no," Lady Edict said, "I'm here to help out. You know, on the farm."

"I don't rightly see what a lass like you could do," Mr. Fake said, "even if it were socially acceptable."

"Well, what needs doing?" The back porch fell off with a crash. "Besides that, of course."

"This stump needs pulling," Mrs. Fake said, fixing on something she was sure the coddled aristocrat couldn't accomplish. "But we've already tried Jenkins' horse Hercules, and he couldn't budge it."

Glowing, Lady Edict held up her mitts, yanking off her kid gloves finger by finger. "Percy, hold these."

"M'lady," I whispered, "I don't know what you're planning, but perhaps Mr. Crawly ought to draw up a waiver or something? In case of injury?"

Lady Edict rolled her head this way and that, pulled each elbow, stretched out her quads, and jogged in place for a moment.

"M'lady?"

"That won't be necessary, Percy. Stand back, please."

Lady Edict dropped down into a squat, then spread her arms wide, wrapping them around the knotty, deep-rooted trunk. After a few breaths, her muscles clenched—her breath quickened—her cheeks flushed, then filled with air. Puffing like a steam engine, the small woman seemed to grow. Her eyes bulged. The cords on her neck strained. She bellowed…and with one mighty yank, the stump came free, spraying us with clods. We all burst into gobsmacked applause.

"Quit clapping and tell me—unh!—where you want it?"

"Just throw it on the tip," Mrs. Fake said. "We'll burn it."

After it was done, and we were on our way back to Downturn, I asked Lady Edict had she'd accomplished the feat.

"Simple," she said, smiling quietly. "I imagined I was ripping off Lady Marry's head."

•   •   •

On the way home, we stopped by the hospital, as Lady Edict had pulled every muscle in her body. While she sat, submerged neck-deep in liniment, I spied Dhumbas, sitting on the edge of a soldier's bed, deep in private conversation. Naturally I listened.

"My god," I heard the evil ex-footman say, "I wouldn't have thought it possible. You're even more bitter than I am."

"Are you blind, too?" the soldier asked.

"No, he's just a pillock," I chimed in.

"Shut your gob," Dhumbas said, backhanding me.

"But I thought you were kind and gentle," the man said in the direction of Dhumbas.

"I am! Completely, ask anyone! That was…just a ghost. You know these old buildings. Haunted, every one."

Just then, Lady Unsybil walked by, her outstretched arms denoting 3:19. "This place is haunted? No way I'm staying here! We should move the hospital up to the Abbey or something."

"Yes, we should!" Dhumbas said. "Why don't you go suggest it to Major Clarkson?"

"I will! He and Majors Hammond and May are racing electrified push-chairs from Glasgow to Ripping, but as soon as they get back, I'll say something."

She traipsed away, leaving the three of us.

I said the only thing that seemed appropriate, under the circumstances. "Whooo...WHOO-OOO..." I rather liked being a ghost.

Dhumbas grabbed me by my thing-smock and launched me out of doors. I kept listening, just to spite him.

"Do you think it likely that they'll move us up to the Abbey?" the blind soldier asked.

"I'd expect so, yes," Dhumbas said. "That voice you heard was the Earl's youngest daughter. She isn't very bright, but they dote on her. If she asks, it'll happen."

"I see," said Dhumbas' new friend. The lieutenant seemed nice, so I wanted to warn him about Dhumbas' ability to muddle everything. There would be time for that—or so I thought.

"If we're going to live in style," Dhumbas' new friend said jauntily, "I guess I'd better shave."

"I don't think that's a very good idea," Dhumbas replied. "Put down that straight razor."

"My beard came in at ten years of age," he said lightly. "I can do it by feel. It'll be fine, you'll see."

It wasn't. Oh god, how it wasn't.

● ● ●

After the squalor of the farm and the gory death at the hospital, the genteel insanity of a dinner at Downturn came as a comparative relief. Though even that tranquil setting I thought might erupt into fisticuffs, once Lady Violent and Sir Richard Baldlisle descended into conversation. You may remember Sir Richard's famous serial, *"The Huns Under Your Bed!"* which brought so much sober clarity and well-reasoned discourse to the months leading up to the War. Unfortunately, since then his papers had taken a turn towards the sensationalist. Lady Violent was not a fan.

"We have only been talking a short while," the Dowager Countess declared, "and I feel I *must* call you Sir Dick."

"I am glad you feel you know me so well."

"I don't."

As usual, her ladyship swung in to the rescue, snagging a spare demitasse cup from my third left side pocket. "Sir Richard, I wonder if you might tell us about your latest venture?"

"With pleasure, Lady Cantswim. It's a special service where people can write their particulars on a piece of paper…"

"What kind of people? What particulars?" Lady Violent sniffed.

"Why, anyone."

"Not interested," the Dowager Countess snapped.

"—where they live, what they like, whatever they're doing at the moment—"

Lady Edict saw bold new vistas for her epistolary mayhem. "You mean, like, 'I am having coffee after-dinner, YUM'?"

"Exactly," the tycoon said. "Then, for a small fee, my service will copy that piece of paper and deliver it to everyone you know. And you'll receive all their slips of paper. And you can update it whenever you like."

"So," said the Earl, "instead of actually doing the things you like, you'll spend your entire life filling out forms."

"That's about the size of it."

"My god," his lordship said, "what an utter waste of time."

Lady Violent concurred. "I may not know much about this modern world, but I know retarded when it see it, and that is retarded."

"Granny," Lady Unsybil tut-tutted, "the medical term is 'cretinous.' Or is it 'Mongoloid'? I always mix up my soon-to-be offensive labels."

"Mongoloid, retarded, cretinous, that's as may be," Sir Dick shrugged, "but it's quite popular so far. We've tested it extensively."

"On prisoners of war I hope?" Lady Violent quavered. "What's the name, so I can avoid it like the plague?"

Sir Dick flashed a lupine smile. "I'd tell you, but then I'd have to sue you."

• • •

That night before bed, I was slumped in a corner, half-asleep. It had been a long day, as they all were for me at Downturn. As Wanna dug various hair-care products out of my right back compartments, I drifted in and out of consciousness.

Lady Marry's voice floated up like a vapor. "Is that how it is with you and Mr. Baits?"

"Mr. Baits and I are like—we're like—" Wanna paused, then looked at Lady

Marry through the mirror. "Imagine if you had a child, and it was turned into a powder, and you could sprinkle it over all your food. Would you ever use salt again? Or if that child were made of leather, and you could make shoes out of it, or lederhosen..."

I dozed. When Lady Marry spoke sharply, my ears pricked:

"...But Wanna, it's not that simple for someone like me. I have blood on my hands. Well, not my hands, exactly."

"That's no reason to settle, m'lady..."

Dozed off again. When I came back, Lady Marry's head was full of beads. "I don't think I like cornrows."

"Wear them for a few days, m'lady. See if they grow on you."

"Oh, all right...Don't think I'm being noble by marrying Sir Dick, because I'm not. It's purely self-interest."

"If it's about the money, I can understand."

"No, it's not that," Marry said. "Baldlisle's in love with his work. What we'll have together—all we'll have—is a nice, long, thoroughly loveless marriage. That's the only way I won't end up in the dock for murder."

Wanna had a thought. "Lady Marry, have you ever considered—experimenting?"

"My word, Wanna! This book is racy enough as it is!"

"No, no, m'lady, not with me. There's a certain woman I'd like getting rid of..."

At that point, the conversation strayed above my pay-grade, so I let myself drift off to sleep for good.

CHAPTER TEN.

His Majesty's Lip-Restiffening Station #14
(July 1917)

People ask me now, did I mind when Downturn Abbey changed into His Majesty's Lip-Restiffening Station #14? Mind? It was the best thing that had happened to me for years! In my spare moments, I could always pick up a penny or two delivering messages between bedridden Tommies. "Lend us a fag," "Stay away from my Lil!" things like that. With warriors in close quarters, feuds always spring up, and I made quite a bit from all that back-and-forth. And when a cloud of Christian brotherhood would uncharacteristically descend, I wasn't above stirring the pot myself.

"Pardon me, sir, but that gentleman over there in the eyepatch says you cut and run at Hill 60. Says he saw it."

"Oh, he does, does he? Take a message! 'Dear Cyclops—"

But apart from that, for old Percy, things didn't change much. I was still thing-boy, dragging my smock-full of paraphernalia hither and yon. I still had to haul Lady Edict's bloody great piles of mail down to the village twice a day. (Now she was writing the Huns.)

She and I were picking our way through a forest of beds towards the front door, when we came upon a young man weeping as if his heart were about to burst. Eventually she would become hard—we all would—but at this point such sights were still new at Downturn, so Lady Edict had to ask. "Why are you crying?"

The soldier held up a letter. "It's from my girl. She just gave me the Order of the Boot."

"What's that mean?" I asked.

"She dumped me," the soldier blubbered.

"That's preposterous," Lady Edict said. "Whatever for?"

The soldier revealed a bandaged stump where a hand used to reside.

Edict was outraged. "Any woman who'd do that, doesn't deserve you."

"I know," the soldier said. "I know it's for the best."

"Then why are you crying?"

"Because it's the hand that I wank with."

Lady Edict blushed crimson, and I had to stamp my own foot to keep from laughing. But what Lady Edict did next showed spunk, so to speak. Sitting down, she declared, "Then I will be your hand—what do you say to that?"

"A great lady like you?"

"Let's write her a letter, you and I. Shall we do that?"

"You'd do that for me?"

"Certainly I would. I write nasty letters all the time. In fact, I send loads of 'em a day to the Boche. 'Dear Johann' stuff, I call them all the most dreadful names. So you are in excellent, erm, hand. Now, then"—she uncapped her pen and adjusted the blank page—"Shall we start off with the c-word, or would you like to hold that in reserve for later?"

The soldier was shocked. "I didn't know grand ladies like you used such language."

"Oh please," Lady Edict said. "Obviously you don't have sisters."

•   •   •

Of course, no one familiar with Miss O'Lyin could be shocked by the c-word. She would've hit the bricks ages ago, had she worked anywhere else but Downturn Abbey. The Cantswims had a very odd view of their staff; the decent ones usually got fired or left, while the bad apples sat there rotting for decades. Her ladyship explained it to me once. "Percy, when someone is rotten, when they take you for granted, that's when you must be most loyal to them. That's what being a Cubs fan is all about."

"Yes, m'lady," I nodded, as if I'd understood a word.

The rest of the household, upstairs and down, were endlessly fascinated by Miss O'Lyin's apparently mystical power over her employer. One night, Wanna, Lady Marry and I sat in Lady Marry's bedroom, trying out yet another hairstyle. The cornrows had been a failure—Sir Dick didn't find them "feminine" enough. So this time, Wanna was frizzing her hair out into what would now be called "an Afro."

"I'm not kidding," Wanna said. "I think we ought to stage an intervention."

"Oh Lord," Lady Marry said, "I remember when we had to do that for Granny. She was utterly devoted to Dr. Osbert's Toddler Suppressant."

Wanna glanced up. "That was before my time, thank god."

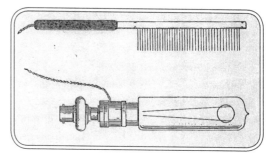

Downturn was the first great house to employ that fantastic blurt of modernity, the hot comb.

"Papa still has a scar on his hand from where she bit him." Lady Marry looked at me through the mirror. "So, you walked into Mama's bedroom while she was with her Gaelic Svengali. Then what did Mama say, thing-boy?"

"She said, 'I agree Dhumbas would make a fine Prime Minister, but first we have to get him back to Downturn.'"

"Ye gods."

"It's like, if you had a child—"

Lady Marry cut her off. "No more metaphors, Wanna. You cannot handle them responsibly."

"We'd better change the subject, then. I don't think I can stop myself."

"Fair enough. Tell me again how you saw Mr. Baits?"

"Well, m'lady, I was down in the village, helping thing-boy here take Lady Edict's correspondence. That girl has logorrhea."

"Impossible," Lady Marry said. "Lady Edict has never gotten past third-base. Were any of the letters about me?"

"I doubt it, m'lady."

"Percy?"

"No, m'lady. All the envelopes said, "Huns, c/o The War, Europe.'"

Wanna teased a lock out to preposterous lengths. "Do any of those actually get delivered?"

"Who cares? It keeps her out of trouble," Marry said. "Is this hairstyle working, do you think? Seems rather Hebraic."

"It's a definite look, m'lady. I'll keep practicing. Anyway, we were coming out of the post office, and there, at the pub across the road, was Mr. Baits. He was writing on one of those little signs, in chalk."

"Heavens," Lady Marry said. "What did it say? Some protestations of love?"

"'Karaoke every Wed,'" I said, as if it were only yesterday (it had been the day before that). "'Fairer Sex No Cover. Anti-Heineken Rally Thu!'"

"No cover charge, you say?"

"I was flabbergasted," Wanna said. "Mr. Baits, working at The Slap and Tickle!"

The Slap and Tickle was notorious, a fly-specked, down-at-the-heel place for strangers to temporarily couple. "No better than behind the bicycle shed," Mrs. Snughes said. At one time, it had been quite respectable; then the war came, and things changed. Such places had become terrifically popular, now that the Western Front was making new singles everyday. It was the center of Ripping's thriving "hookup culture," and here our Mr. Baits had landed. Every evening, he dispensed alcohol and bad ideas; every morning, he swept out broken glass, spew and regret.

"So what are you going to do next?" Lady Marry asked.

"Go see him, I suppose."

"You are brave."

"Not really, m'lady," Wanna said. "It's more like, if you had a child, and—"

"*Wanna!*"

•   •   •

That next Wednesday, Wanna asked me to accompany her.

"From thing-boy to wing-boy," I said, feeling a tiny rise in the world.

"Nah," Wanna said. "It's just that no one will proposition me if they think you're my kid."

I agreed, of course. I had nothing better to do and, truth be told, I had become a bit of an historian for all the emotional tumult at Downturn. If Wanna hadn't invited me, I'd been toying with the idea of appearing in disguise.

So there we were, waiting in the damp, a thirtysomething housemaid and her 13-year-old wing-boy. When Wanna and I boarded the bus to Ripping, we quite accidentally sat behind Ethyl and her new beau, Major Mistake. I could tell he was trouble, just from his surname.

"Let's give them privacy," Wanna said, listening intently. I nodded, and did the same.

"How's about I seduce you," the soldier said, "get you with child, then completely dodge my responsibilities?"

Ethyl giggled at the oily creature. "I bet you say that to all the girls."

"I'm serious, Ethyl—I think I can make you the unhappiest girl in the world. If you'll only let me try."

"I can't listen to anymore," Wanna whispered, and we got off at the next stop. "It's disgusting," she said. "It's like she's his puppy dog."

I cleared my throat meaningfully, and the maid gave me a look. "Allergies," I croaked. "Hunweed."

During the short walk to the bar, Wanna asked me if I'd ever been to such a place. I said that I had not.

"Good. Keep it that way. The only kinds of men that go into The Slap and Tickle are people like Major Mistake back there."

"And Mr. Baits."

"He's doing something noble. I just know it."

• • •

When we walked in, Mr. Baits was very nobly standing atop the bar, selflessly shirtless and altruistically gyrating to loud music.

"*Who wants to have a fête?*" Mr. Baits bellowed.

"WE DO!" the patrons shouted back.

As the brass band played, Mr. Baits took two bottles of liquor and poured them all over himself. Then he took the bottles, and walked up and down the bar, pouring booze into the open mouths of the patrons who, though they were already drunk, shouted and stamped for more. Wanna and I stood in the darkness of the doorway, I mesmerized, she horrified. Mr. Baits' doughy form pranced and cavorted, straddling the pole at bar's end quite graphically.

"Percy, tell me those aren't backless chaps."

"Only if you tell me Mr. Baits isn't giving that bloke a body shot."

It seemed like the song would never end—to this day, I can never listen to "Lloyd George's Beer" without getting a little sick to my stomach. But just as the band cranked into the final verse, Mr. Baits abruptly stopped scrubbing his nipples—he'd seen Wanna. Suddenly sheepish, Mr. Baits got down off the bar, which was flaming now. He put it out with a bar rag, and signaled the other barman that he wanted to go on break.

I don't know what they said—Wanna made me wait outside—but based on what happened next, I know one thing for sure: Wanna had no room to call Ethyl anyone's puppy dog.

• • •

Manson had been acting squirrelly all day. There was nothing so very unusual about that; what was unusual was how Wanna and I had seen him on the road to Ripping that morning, using the car to nudge along a very reluctant cow.

We discussed it on the ride back. "He's up to something, no mistake."

"Thank god," I replied. "Finally something will happen in this chapter."

"Just what do you mean by that? I saw Mr. Baits. And spoke to him!"

"And licked booze off his chest."

"Quite right," Wanna said indignantly. "That's not nothing."

"Totally expected," I yawned.

Wanna leaned back in her seat. "You're mighty cheeky for a thing-boy."

"Can't help it," I said. "It's how I've been written."

• • •

I didn't have time to give Manson a second thought; there was another dinner at Downturn, this time for the celebrated General Nutt and his staff. After spending a tedious afternoon trailing Dr. Clarkson and Mrs. Crawly through every nook and cranny of the Lip-Stiffening Station, General Nutt took his revenge at dinner, boring the table with the tactics that he'd used at Futilité Ridge.

"…so instead of fighting the Germans, or indeed opposing them in any way, we simply swung open, like a gate."

"But didn't that bother the French?" the Earl asked.

"Sod the French," General Nutt said. "If they don't like it, we'll switch sides."

"Hear, hear," Lady Violent said. "No difference between them and the Italians, I say. Italians are practically Greeks, who are practically Arabs, who are practically Negroes."

"And where do the Jews come in, Granny?" Edict said.

"I am suspicious of all ecru-complected peoples."

"Mama, please," the Earl said. "Go on, General."

"Once Jerry realized that no one was shooting at them, they took off at quite terrific speed into the rear, drinking, looting, having their way with the local women—"

"Which, obviously, we'd been doing for years," Lady Cantswim surmised.

"Quite," General Nutt said, "so no harm done. After several hours of this, none of the German soldiers were in any condition to fight any more. So we just flowed in from either side, and captured them all."

GENERAL NUTT
enlivened the evening with his
unique rendition of "Tipperary."

"But it seems rather…unsporting," Sir Dick said. "And bad copy, besides."

"Unsporting?" Captain Crawly replied. "Ten thousand Jerrys captured without firing a shot? If that's unsporting, give me more of it."

"And after we've beaten them, thanks to General Nutt, we can play them all in rugger," Lady Marry said.

"Unfortunately, I'm afraid Haig agrees with Sir Dick," General Nutt said sadly. "If we could employ these tactics across a broad front, I have no doubt the Germans would be incapacitated by tea-time. But—"

General Nutt was interrupted by a *furore* to his rear. Mr. Cussin, Mrs. Snughes, and Wanna were all tussling with Manson who, for such a weedy sort, was surprisingly strong.

Thinking quickly, I grabbed the lid of the tray Manson was holding, and socked him over the head with it, stunning him quite thoroughly.

We all looked at the entrée with horror. It was a beef patty between two slices of bun, garnished with tomatoes and lettuce. So that was what the cow'd been for!

"He was going to serve that to the general, m'lord," Mr. Cussin gasped.

"That's what I think of your bloody war!" Manson spat. "I know how you blighters love your cows! If only you loved men—"

Lady Cantswim reached over and grabbed the sandwich. "How I've craved one of these. If anyone doesn't mind…?"

"Cola—perhaps the General—" Lord Cantswim looked at Nutt, who was smiling broadly.

"Eat it with my compliments. And let him go."

Manson shrugged off Mr. Cussin, madder than ever.

"My dear fellow," the General said, "that's Hindu. Totally different. I have no special feelings about cows whatever."

•　•　•

After Manson had stomped off, and the footmen had gone to get the pudding, General Nutt said, "I have an announcement to make. During our tour of the facility this afternoon, several soldiers took me aside, and told me of someone whose simple acts of kindness have made their stay more comfortable. None of them would ever reveal exactly what these acts were, but how they said it—the looks of genuine gratitude—was testament enough. So—"

General Nutt raised his glass, and most of the table tensed for praise.

"—here's to Lady Edict. May that pesky tennis elbow of yours heal very soon."

•　•　•

That night, I stood by the Lord and Lady Cantswims' matrimonial bed, the front pockets of my smock filled with various stomach preparations.

"Can you imagine Manson's behavior?" his lordship said crossly.

"Oh, the hamburger wasn't bad," Lady Cantswim said. "I'm just not used to them topped in shamrocks."

"But I should fire him, shouldn't I? First that affair with Unsybil—"

"Robber! Don't read ahead!"

"What? I only meant the brawl in Ripping. What did you mean?"

"Nothing." Lady Cantswim reached over and fished out some Eno Fruit Salts from my smock. "Good night."

$\bullet$ $\bullet$ $\bullet$

One of the most important jobs someone in service can undertake is providing an alibi for their employer. So when the Earl needed an excuse to go down and see Mr. Baits at The Slap and Tickle, I played along. Fifteen minutes later, his lordship, Mr. Baits and I were all slung into a booth, sampling the sweetness of drinking in the afternoon.

"I told Cola I needed to inoculate Percy against the evils of the world," his lordship said, "starting with 'Wet Petticoat Mondays.'"

Mr. Baits smiled. "I miss her ladyship. Did she believe you?"

"Probably not, but she didn't stop me either…Baits, it's not the same without you. Boring isn't the word for it."

"Downturn, boring? I cannot believe it."

The Earl wiped a fleck of beer off his forehead. The buxom barmaid in the cutoff bloomers prancing across the bar wasn't dancing as much as spraying. Petticoats hold a lot of liquid.

"Nor I. But it's so bad, Mrs. Snughes has taken to prowling the corridors at night, seeing if she can catch one of the maids *in flagrante delicto.*"

"Has she?"

"Yes, as a matter of fact."

Concern flicked across the valet's face. "It wasn't Wanna, was it?"

"Of course not. So, Baits—will you return to Downturn?"

"If you think it'll help the plot, m'lord."

"I'd say. They've got us singing songs to fill time. Next episode, I expect I'll be required to leap a tank of dangerous fish or something."

"I didn't realize, m'lord. Of course I'll come."

"Good man."

Mr. Baits saw me ogling the barmaid. "Steady on, Percy."

"Quite right, both hands on the table," his lordship said.

"And Mr. Crawly, he hasn't been able to drive the story?"

"One man can only do so much. The good news is, I think it's possible for Killem to be assigned his batman."

"Soldier-servant's a good position."

"It is. My concern, however, is that Killem has a funny conception of the job."

"What do you mean, m'lord?"

His lordship sipped his bitter. "It's probably nothing. It's just that—Killem keeps talking about his uniform, endlessly. And how this is his opportunity to become a hero."

"I think every soldier feels that way. I certainly did," Mr. Baits said. "The Front will sort him out."

"That's one way to put it," I said quietly.

Smarting over the imbroglio with General Nutt, Manson switched tactics and attempted to mind-control Downturn's animals. "Local ruminant! You are under my total and complete power!"

Modern dance at Ypres, 1915.

"We Are All Geese" event, 1916

Refugees flee rather than see Poseurs show, Ghent 1917.

CHAPTER ELEVEN.

The Caped Crusader
(1918)

O ne evening, as the men relaxed in the library and I stood silently in the corner, his lordship beckoned me to him. As he placed the cigar clippers back in my top right pocket, he said, "Percy, I'd like you to accompany Killem to Flanders. Not permanently, just make sure he ends up in the right place. You've been there."

"I have been there, m'lord, which is why I'd prefer to let the Army handle it."

"I'd feel better if you made sure."

Sir Dick piped up. Seventeen whiskies in, he was in a mellow mood—or maybe he was worried that Lady Marry liked me better than him. "Tell you what, why don't you go over there as my correspondent? Write down what you see, and I'll pay you handsomely for it."

"M'lord—Sir Richard—it's not that I'm not grateful—"

"Come on, man! He's an Earl, and I'm a millionaire! What are you trying to do, break the whole class system?"

So I went.

• • •

On this side: the loyal, clean, brave, honest, reverent lads of "The King's Own Poseurs." A hundred yards away: the fearsome, spike-helmed Boche. And yet God poured an equal measure of sunshine down upon each, clarifying His thoughts on the subject. For once, both sides seemed to get the memo; so far that day hostilities had been sporadic—a crump of shellfire simply to mark every quarter-hour, and when one side's machine guns chattered, their opposites responded, but only out of politeness.

One man, however, had other plans.

I was asleep in the dugout shared by Captain Crawly and his soldier-servant Killem, having a bit of kip before heading back to Blighty. After morning stand-to, Killem had crept back inside and, without waking me, switched his Army togs for something of his own manufacture: a pair of grey tights, a long black cape, and a bright yellow belt jingling with tools and canisters. Now, Killem stood on the fire-step, adjusting his hood.

"*For those who trod Evil's path,*

And chose a life of crime
Are about to feel the Batman's wrath
And—blast! I stink at rhyme."

Twenty feet down the trench, Captain Crawly was talking with a brother officer.

"Morning, Squiffy. How goes the interpretive dance?"

Captain Reginald Squiffington Frigiped had been working on a piece called "The Big Push" for as long as anyone could remember. While no one expected him to finish, but it was considered good form to ask.

"Not half bad—though I expect to be savaged by the critics."

Captain Crawly made a supportive noise. "'Genius in its own time,' old boy."

"I say, Crawly, your batman's an odd duck."

"Family friend," Captain Crawly mumbled. "I promised someone I'd take him on. Don't worry, Squiffy, he does this every morning."

"What are those pointy things?"

"I think they're supposed to be ears…Blimey, he's going over!"

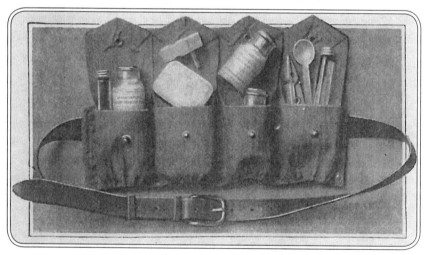

Killem's "utility belt."

Captain Crawly sprinted down the trench, but only grabbed air. Killem was now galumphing across no-man's-land at a dead run, shouting something about "evildoers."

Captain Crawly couldn't bear to watch. But then—a miracle happened. There were no explosions, no chatter of death. The Germans were *laughing*.

"Die Fliedermaus!"

"Ach, das ist so lustig ich Scheisse!"

Captain Crawly saw his opportunity. Taking the ladder in two steps, with his white handkerchief over his head, he ran into the open. Killem was about twenty yards away, trying to unsnag his long black cape from a bit of wire.

As Killem kneeled there in the mud, the delighted Germans rained empty food tins down on him.

"Just you wait, evildoers…Stupid wire…" Killem paused to throw a homemade boomerang at the nearest group of hysterical soldiers. It scribbled through the air harmlessly.

"Don't shoot! Don't shoot! *Ist ein dummkopf! Geficken in der head!*" Captain Crawly skidded to a stop. "Killem, what the blazes are you doing?"

"Ridding the world of evildoers, obviously… Stupid cape!"

"Forget the bloody cape!" He tore it off, removing Killem's flannel cowl, too.

"Spiffing, sir! Now everyone knows my secret identity!"

• • •

Hearing the commotion, I stumbled out of the dugout, just in time to see Squiffy spring to attention. Ambling down our trench was Muggins, Colonel and noted prig.

"At ease, Captain…How's your dancing whatsit?"

"Very well, sir, thank you."

"I say, are those our men out there?"

"Yes, Colonel Muggins."

"And—no one's shooting at them?"

"Seems not, sir."

"Why not?"

"I…I suppose they find it amusing, sir."

The Colonel's eyes flashed. "Do you find the activities of our unit amusing, Frigiped?"

"No sir…Maybe they're showing mercy, sir."

The Colonel's slow burn burst into full flame. ""The cheek! How in blazes are we supposed to hold a proper war when people act like that?"

Colonel Muggins pushed past the Captain and mounted the fire-step. "*Achtung*, Boche!" He waved his arms, and pointed at the struggling pair. "Bang-bang! At them!"

But the Germans just laughed harder, and Squiffy laughed, too, when something on Killem's belt went off, sending a plume of purple gas all over.

Colonel Muggins was livid. He wheeled on his subordinate. "If this war loses steam, Frigiped, I will hold you personally responsible. What do you intend to do about it?"

The chuckle died in Squiffy's throat. He grabbed a Mills bomb out of a nearby sack; if he could get it near them, but not too near—"Sorry, chaps…"

• • •

At the exact moment the Mills bomb denoted, back at Downturn Abbey, Lady Marry dropped a teacup…

…Craisy sneezed into the lamb stew;

…Lady Edict's hand fell asleep;

…and Lady Unsybil scared the daylights out of two soldiers playing ping-pong. "BONG! BONG! BONG!" she yelled. *Thirteen* times.

• • •

The Earl looked at the unruly knot of family and staff, all in nightclothes, all yawning and scratching, and rubbing sleep from their eyes. "I've just received a telegram saying Dratyew Crawly and Killem have been wounded."

"Both of them at the same time?" asked Mr. Cussin.

His lordship nodded. "Apparently they're doing it in bulk now, to save money."

Her ladyship turned yawn-face into shock-face. "Wounded? Are you sure?"

"Yes, I thought they were merely missing," the Dowager Countess quavered.

"We're skipping that episode, Granny," Lady Edict said. "Bit slow."

"I may be old-fashioned, but where I come from, we don't skip—"

"Well, you'd better get used to it," Lady Marry said, "unless you'd rather hear more Home Rule folderol from the chauffeur."

"Helps sell the show in America," Mr. Cussin rumbled.

"Along those lines," Lady Violent said, "I find it odd that Unsybil is without a paramour. Do you feel she is a Lebanese?"

Wanna spoke up. "Perhaps if we were on Showtime, m'lady."

"I only wish she were," Lady Marry said. "As it is we must live and die with the employment opportunities of Marley the sub-valet, and the breathtaking establishment of a local soup-kitchen."

"Ye gods!" Lady Violent yelped. "Is there no fresh incident in this story? We must get Mr. Crawly and Killem back to Downturn at once!"

"But that's impossible," Lady Cantswim said.

"Nothing is impossible for the English upperclasses! *Hand me the phone!*"

I looked at the Earl for confirmation. "Do it, Percy. And stand back."

I was grateful for the warning, for what occurred next was a hurricane, albeit one of the most genteel kind. (It smelled like tuberose.)

"Hello, Wimpy? It's your Aunt...No, the other one, the one that's still alive...I realize it's late, but I need a favor. Two friends are wounded. A Captain Crawly, and his batman, Killem...Yes, we must have them recuperating here with us...I know...I realize that...He may well be a lunatic, but he's our lunatic... Yes, of course...Wimpy, it's clearly been too long since you've been here—if one applied such stringent standards to Downturn, there'd be no one left....I am aware of that...Of course it won't be easy, the question is, is there a class system here or not?...But 'everyone' is not asking. I am asking. What if 'everyone' was your Aunt? You'd be some sort of polyglot monster...Don't make me come down to London, don't make me do it. I *will* break out the Ugly Parasol—oh I forgot, you went to Beton, you would probably enjoy that...My dear Wimpy, at the end of the day, it's simply a matter of sets. We don't have the money for more of them. What do you think this is, HBO?"

With that, Lady Violent won the day. Replacing the receiver, she turned to the group. "It is done. Both will be staying here." Amid sighs of gratitude, she shuffled towards the door. "And, since we are skipping things, might we have fewer heart-warming stories of bridging the Great Divide? It runs roughshod over my digestion."

Killem gave me this sketch of his "batmobile."

• • •

The return of Captain Crawly and Killem, while undoubtedly a good thing, carried with it a measure of sadness. For one thing, the Captain was having a dreadful time with the string in his legs, and it seemed certain he would miss all the Jitterbuggery so fervently predicted by *Lo!*. For another, poor Killem was even worse: the force of the explosion had lodged a scrap of cape so deeply in his windpipe that he wheezed and gurgled like a broken Electrolux.

The bards of old were right when they sang:

War!
Hunh!
What is it good for?
Absolutely nothing!
Say it again!

Several days after Downturn's heir had returned, I stood beside a weeping Lineolia Sweeper, as she plucked hankie after hankie from my smock.

As she gave a loud honk, the door opened and Lady Marry walked in.

"Oh! I am sorry, Lineolia."

"It's all right."

"Why are you crying?"

"Dratyew's called off the engagement. He says we can never be properly married."

"But that's absurd!" Marry said. "Take my word for it, if the C of E can consecrate someone like me, you and Cousin Dratyew should be no problem."

"It's not that," Lineolia whispered. "Dr. Clarkson said he's impotent."

"Dr. Clarkson says a lot of things, and you believe him at your own risk… Perhaps Cousin Dratyew misheard him. Perhaps he said Dratyew's 'important.' He is the heir again."

"No, he said 'impotent.' I'm sure of it."

"Or maybe he was admitting that he, the doctor, was impotent? Big, blustery chaps are always the ones that let you down."

"I wouldn't know. All I can say is that Dratyew says we cannot be together, so he's sent me away."

"He's being silly," Marry said. "Papa has books on his special shelf, way up at the top, which I've studied intensely. Legs or no legs, there's loads of things you can do. For example, if you take these two fingers, and place them between—"

Lineolia cut her off. "I know you're just trying to help, Marry, but you're squicking me out."

• • •

Things were going no better for Downturn's other star-crossed lovers, Wanna and Mr. Baits. I was able to track their affairs rather precisely, because every time Mr. Baits walked down to Ripping, I had to accompany him carrying a prodigious quantity of lubricant. It was really awful, that belt. Somewhere, Torquemada was giggling.

But Mr. Baits wasn't, because this day, halfway from Downturn, I'd run out of grease, and every step became a world of chafing. So as he and Wanna stood in front of the altar, praying, tear after tear rolled down his broad cheeks.

"Are you…crying for us?" she asked.

"Praying for the key," he said hoarsely. The belt screeched with every move.

"What about Killem and Captain Crawly?"

"Sod those two, my inner thighs are hamburger."

"Well, send the thing-boy for talc or something. You're too big to carry back." Wanna leaned in. "And when he's gone, we can—"

"But how? The belt…"

"Being Lady Marry's maid has its benefits. It's like going to Uni."

"Is she really…lethal?"

"She believes so. Anyway, you can't imagine the things she's dug up. For example, you can take your elbow, and—"

Mr. Baits saw my uptick in interest, and judged it unwholesome. "Percy, go over to The Slap and Tickle and see if you can scare up some grease. Ask at the bar."

"Take your time!" Wanna added.

I didn't have to be asked twice. Whatever was about to happen next, it was nothing I wished to see (or relate to you). As I shuffled down the aisle in my smock, I overheard Mr. Baits ask, "Didn't there used to be a large stained glass window here?"

"Not after Mr. Crawly saw it. Now, I need to you focus your mind on your big toe."

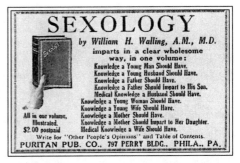

Forced by malign circumstance to educate herself, Lady Marry eventually wrote this book under a pseudonym.

113

"Before we begin, can I just say how glad I am that, out of all the possible nations of the world, England conquered India?"

· · ·

A few days later, Lady Marry was talking to Captain Crawly, who was looking rather green around the gills. "Lineolia tells me that you have thrown her over."

"Not thrown her over. Spared her a long, long ordeal, a marriage in name only, bereft of the physical act of love between a man and woman."

Lady Marry's cheeks flushed. "You might be surprised, Cousin Dratyew. That's just the sort of thing some women dream of."

"Marry, being in the Army gives one fairly good gaydar. No matter what Cousin Violent says, I do not feel that Lady Unsybil—"

"I'm not talking about my sister! I'm talking about m—Lineolia."

"MLineolia? Who's that?"

Lady Marry recovered herself. "It's my pet name for your dear bride, whom you will marry, then be married to. Forever."

"I'm not marrying anyone, Marry. Dr. Clarkson says that the string connecting both my legs has been severed. I am half a man."

"But what a half! Anyway, Dr. Clarkson is an idiot. Last time I saw him, he and his pals were packing an ice truck full of black powder, and trying to push it over the Cliffs of Dover."

"Why?"

"Who knows?" Marry smoothed his sheets. "Female desire is more fluid, Cousin Dratyew. What happens below the waist is secondary to what happens in the head. Or haven't you seen all those awful books Edict's addicted to? *The Seed Broadcaster, Naked Came the Harvester, Born to Be Milked…*"

Captain Crawly leaned over and retched violently.

"I know, that was my reaction, too."

· · ·

Growing up as I did, in the rough-and-tumble of Ripping Foundling Home, my sensibilities were much less delicate than those of my betters; not to put too fine a point on it, the perilous Lady Marry was a chance that I was increasingly willing to take. As one might expect from a boy of 15, I began trailing her ladyship, just on the off-chance that she might want to cross the Great Divide. She never did, but it did make my time at Downturn pass more quickly.

One day soon after The Retching, I was present when Lady Marry ran into

Mr. Baits on the landing at the top of the stairs.

"What a shame about Killem," she said.

"Indeed."

"Still, we all knew with a name like that, he'd go sooner rather than later. Did you enjoy the wedding?"

"I did, m'lady. Though I found the decorations to be a bit...eccentric."

"I thought Craisy looked quite nice as batgirl. Though the enormous penny did tend to dominate the bedroom," Lady Marry said. ""Something happened to Killem's mind over there. But you know war, Baits. I needn't tell you what it does to people."

"Was there something your ladyship needed?" Mr. Baits said. "Otherwise, I think Wanna's got a new lock-picking set she's anxious to try."

"I'll let you get to it then, Baits. Only—I just wanted to say, there's no need to worry about Genghis. Sir Dick's taken care of my sordid past. Though part of me says I should've been brave and bared my soul."

"And plunge the house into scandal? I'm glad you didn't."

"Well, you didn't see how much *Naughty Ladies Magazine* offered. I would've had November's super-extendable rotogravure all to myself."

They laughed, then Lady Marry's smile faded. "Still, Baits, you should know that Genghis was angry. She made the most awful threats. Her head spun around, and she dampened the floor of Sir Dick's office."

"That sounds like her. Thank you for the warning, m'lady."

"Baits, I hope you don't think me overstepping, but—why on Earth did you marry her?"

Downturn's paunchy Lothario sighed deeply. "Never, ever use a cut-rate matrimonial agency."

CHAPTER TWELVE.

Lady Edict Gets A Head
(August - November 1918)

Lady Marry pushed Captain Crawly around Downturn's undulating hillocks in a wheelchair. I trailed behind them, hiding behind rocks and trees, and where there were none of those, crawling on my belly. The grass stains aroused strong comment from Mr. Cussin, but Sir Dick was paying me a packet to listen in.

"This whole Downturn ordeal has been a farce," Captain Crawly said, "and it's time to call an end to it. All I am—all I ever wanted to be—is a simple omnibus-chaser."

"So you will go back to Manchester. What then?"

"I will sue them, Marry. I will sue the governments of the world for a million, billion, killion dollars, for the unlawful severance of my leg-strings."

"Forgive me for being ignorant, but what's a 'killion'?"

"I learned about it from a Major Frazier in France. It's a legal term, meaning 'so much money it would kill you to possess it.'"

"Don't see the point of that."

"A killion minus one, then. Another wheelie, please," Captain Crawly said. "The point is: I can't walk, and someone must pay."

"Beginning with me, apparently," Lady Marry said, grunting with the effort.

Captain Crawly eventually grew so demanding that the Earl hired a man to trundle him about in a special veloci-chair. He delighted in crashing into Sir Dick at high speeds.

• • •

The war dragged on, hanging over everything like a stink, making itself felt in innumerable ways. The black armbands, the lists of dead, the cruelty to dachshunds. It even ruined one's afternoon tea.

"Don't know what you're complaining about," Mrs. Phatore sang. "Same as it ever was."

"It was never! There was sand in it!"

"That'd be the 'National Sugar,'" she said. "It's good for you. Scrubs you out from top to tail."

I smacked my lips queasily, and recalled my first day at Downturn, when Dhumbas made me eat dirt.

"We all need to make sacrifices," the cook declared. "Or haven't you heard there's a War on?"

"Stop using cheerfulness as a weapon."

"I will when you stop whining. Why don't you go out to the ward and help some people who really have something to complain about?"

• • •

Much as I hated to admit it, Mrs. Phatore was right. Fifteen minutes later, I was plumping pillows for the most badly injured man I'd ever laid eyes upon.

At the beginning of the war, one would see men missing an arm or a leg. The next year, I noticed a peculiar uptick in people missing both arms or both legs. In 1917, people cut off at the waist became terrifically popular. Now, the final stage had been reached: the creature in front of me was just a noggin, swathed in bandages. Surgeons cutting corners, I suppose. By that last year, everyone was doing as little as possible, waiting for the Twenties to arrive.

Anyway, this Captain Head—who appeared to be badly burned as well— was deep in conversation with Lady Edict. I tried not to eavesdrop, out of politeness (and that no one was paying me). But I couldn't help but overhear the gist of what they were saying.

"But don't you recognize me?"

"Be fair," Lady Edict said tremblingly. "A pair of eyeholes can only convey so much."

"Why won't you call me 'Hatrack'? That's my name, isn't it?"

"It seems cruel, under the circumstances."

The soldier's bandages shifted slightly frownward. "You're blaming me for my own misfortune!"

"Truly I'm not, but if you could just remove the bandages—"

"No! I must protect my face. Rolling around is my only means of locomotion."

Captain Head dropped to the floor, and began rolling himself against Lady Edict's shin, over and over. "Believe me. Believe me. Believe me. I'm begging you."

"Please stop," Lady Edict said. "And don't look up my dress."

"You loved me once."

"There was ever so much more of you, then."

"Edict, I can't give you a body, but I can give you—"

"My word! Captain!"

"What? I was going to say, 'utter devotion.'"

"I'm terribly sorry," Lady Edict said, twisting her handkerchief. "When you've lived with my sister Marry, your mind leaps to certain conclusions. Forgive me."

"What about her? Does she believe my story?"

"I'm afraid not."

Captain Head's emotions boiled over. He banged the flimsy table, spraying Bovril. "WHAT ALWAYS SMELLS LIKE BARBEQUE?"

All conversation in the ward abruptly stopped.

"Oh, it's me," Captain Head said quietly. "Sorry."

Cheeks aflame, Lady Edict scooped up her friend and scurried out of the room without meeting anyone's gaze, not even mine.

• • •

Captain Head apparently continued to plead his case, for a week later, I was helping the Earl paste fairies into reconnaissance photos when Lady Edict walked into the library.

"Papa, can I have a word with you?"

"Of course you can. The question is, *may* you?"

Wearing a furious scowl, Lady Edict hefted a massive potted palm and hurled it through the window. "Stop dismissing me! I know I'm not glamorous like Marry or hip like Unsybil—but I'm perfectly attractive! I'm just not TV-attractive!"

"What is it, daughter? Please don't kill me."

"There is a new man in the ward, a Captain Head. He says he is Cousin Onan."

"You know I hate that nickname."

"Hatrack's suddenly much worse. You'll see why."

The Earl put down his mucilage. "Hatrack Crawly drowned on the *Titanic*.

What does Captain…"

"Head. You'll have no trouble remembering it once you meet him."

"What does Captain Head say to that?"

"He has a whole tale, which I believe. But then again, I would. I am needy, neglected and thoroughly miserable."

"Does he look like Hatrack?"

"Impossible to say; his face is covered in bandages."

"I see. Does he act like him, then?"

"I'm afraid he'd need arms for that, in addition to…Papa, the poor man is just a noggin."

"I see," the Earl said. "Edict, I will investigate it. And perhaps his claim is genuine—perhaps this Captain Head is Hatrack, and the heir to Downturn. But you must be prepared: given the amount of screen time devoted to Cousin Dratyew and Marry, I don't like his chances."

"Thank you, Papa."

"You're welcome." His Lordship glanced out the ragged hole where the window had been, and saw the palm-caved motorcar below. Manson was waving his fist and claiming an assassination attempt. "And Edict, please do try not to destroy our home. The next time you're feeling angry, go hold up the North Gallery for a bit. I'm sure the orphans would appreciate it."

• • •

A week later, the family was assembled in the little library for an important announcement.

"I expect you're all wondering why I've asked you here," the Earl said. "It's something of vital import to us all. I should like to combine episodes."

"Again?" the Dowager Countess yelped.

Sir Dick was no happier. "Are we simply to ignore the gripping tale of my impending real estate transaction?"

"Be fair, Papa," Lady Marry agreed, "we must give everyone time to realize that Sir Dick's a bad hat."

His lordship chuckled. "My dear, your fiancé is a self-made man in a show about the landed aristocracy. Of course he's going to be an ass."

"But what about Ethyl, and her baby?" Lady Cantswim asked.

"The father is dead."

"But if the father is dead, Robber, why in blazes did we spend scene after scene with poor Mrs. Snughes hauling herself down to Ripping to commiserate in a garret?"

Edict spoke up. "Speaking of scenes, Papa, Captain Head and I have played several of them—"

"—which all go like this," the Earl replied. "A little small talk from you, then a possibly bogus memory from him, he quavers, you quaver, he complains, you soothe him, and then we cut to Cussin dithering over whether he's switching gigs." The Earl turned to his butler. "You're not, by the way."

"Very good, m'lord. It'll save on locations."

"But Papa, Captain Head is a genuinely interesting storyline. He may be the real heir to Downturn," Edict said.

Captain Crawly piped up. "I believe this is the time where I say something bitter."

"Not necessary, my dear fellow," the Earl said. "This mysterious Head is simply going to leave."

"I don't care what any of you say!" Lady Edict fumed. "He's mine and I'm going to keep him!"

Then Lady Marry spoke. "For once I agree with Edict. Surely there must be some resolution."

"Nope," the Earl said. "He just rolls off down the road, leaving us all to wonder."

Lady Violent was vexed. "He'd never! Not after dragging us through a whole episode. Surely that violates the Geneva Convention as it relates to television?"

"Perhaps it's a seed, planted for next season?" Lady Cantswim offered.

Also cut: a long subplot where Downturn is overrun by rabbits.

"One can only hope," the Earl said. "Who knows what the future holds?"

"I do, and it's going to suck," Captain Crawly declared.

"Dratyew, that'll count for all the rest of your scenes, if you don't mind."

"Fine. Cousin Unsybil, would you mind terribly rolling me back to my room? Goodbye, everyone. Think of me when you wipe your own bottom."

"I already do," said Sir Dick.

"It takes a special gift of personality to make oneself less attractive than a bitter paraplegic," Lady Violent observed.

"And on that chestnut," the Earl said, "I think we're finished here."

The meeting broke up to rampant grumbling. I saw the lady of the house cornering her husband: "Robber, you wouldn't be hurrying through this episode to avoid being caught out in something, would you? With a maid, perhaps?"

"Of course not, Cola. Don't be ridiculous. It's simply narrative expediency... For example, do you know what Isapill does, when you and Violent erect a completely transparent plan to get rid of her?"

"Gives us hell with a plan of her own? Confront us? The woman's annoying, but she's wicked smart, and very headstrong."

"No—she falls for it, hook line and sinker."

"Wow."

The Earl put his hand on his wife's shoulder. "Trust me. This is for the best."

•   •   •

The downstairs staff was still digesting the ramifications of the Earl's decision when Mrs. Snughes appeared. "Mr. Baits, you have a telegram."

"I was hoping we'd skip over this part," he said, ashen-faced.

"Not bloody likely," Miss O'Lyin said.

He read the telegram. "YES!" Then his fist-pump died mid-pump. "Oh, wait..."

Mr. Baits rushed out of the room as quickly as if he'd eaten Mrs. Phatore's trifle. Wanna trailed after.

Later, secreted in the repaired drop-ceiling of Mrs. Snughes' sitting-room, I understood what had happened. "My wife Genghis is dead," Mr. Baits said gravely.

"That's fantastic!"

"That's what I thought," he said, "but there's more. It was death-by-misadventure, we both know that. However, the police are apt to suspect murder—especially in light of Genghis' charming personality."

"Let's focus on the positive, Mr. Baits. I'm sure his lordship will let you go cut the head off, or burn the heart or something. Always best to make sure," Wanna said. "How did she die?"

"Suffocated. She tried to climb through a funnel. They found her with it jammed over her nose and mouth, and a determined look on her face."

"I don't understand."

"It's like a little child in the bath, being afraid he's going to go down the plughole," Mr. Baits explained. "Genghis simply cannot—could not—judge size and distance."

"But surely that's not your fault?"

"I bought the funnel," Mr. Baits said. "It was months ago, for baking. But no one would believe that, not now."

"Go to the police! Tell them! Today!"

"I can't," Mr. Baits said.

"You know, I really think you like being falsely accused," Wanna said. "You don't tell me things, you don't tell his lordship things, you don't confide in Mr. Cussin or Mrs. Snughes—what does all this secrecy get you? What does it bring anyone besides misery?"

I leaned forward to hear the answer—and fell through the ceiling again.

"Percy," Mr. Baits said, "you'd better find another hiding place. They're going to start taking it out of your wages."

• • •

Captain Crawly's war injury had turned him from the putative Earl of Cantswim to the mean dog tied up in the backyard. Everyone at Downturn—family and staff—learned to give him plenty of space. Sir Dick, however, could not resist an opportunity to tease his one-time rival.

One evening after dinner, he and Captain Crawly were by the fire in the library. "Do you know what Marry and I are going to do on our honeymoon?" Sir Dick said, smiling coldly. *"We're going to use our legs."*

Quick as a flash, Captain Crawly's right foot shot out and kicked his tormentor solidly on the shin.

"Aggh!" Sir Dick fell to the ground. The plutocrat's swearing was loud enough to rouse the rest of the family, which rushed in to see what had happened.

Sir Dick hauled himself up from the carpet. Hands on knees he sputtered, "Lord Cantswim! This sharp-footed little git has just kicked me in the shin!"

Captain Crawly was unrepentant. "Come closer and I'll kick you in the nose."

"Dratyew, my boy, is this true?" By way of answer, Captain Crawly's left foot gave his lordship the same treatment.

"Aggh! That's...wonderful!" the Earl gasped. "Everyone, come see what Dratyew can do! He's recovered!"

In a trice, everyone, from Lady Violent to Dr. Clarkson were on the floor, writhing in happiness. "Permission to say 'cock' in this parody," Dr. May gasped.

No one was happier than Lineolia, whose future had changed from decades of griping and unwilling sitz-baths, to as much bloodline-extending as she could bear. "My dear, I'm so happy you've recovered! We can do anything! We can even 'get married'! Please note the quotes."

"Yes, you'll be able to 'get married,' and everything else besides," Dr. Clarkson said, blinking back tears. "But if you ever do that to me again, I'm going to strap you into a Hispano-Suiza and drop you from a bloody great height!"

●　●　●

Though Captain Crawly's physical recovery was a cause for genuine celebration, the resurrection of his marriage to Lineola was another story. Though Lady Cantswim complained constantly about the expense, no one was unhappier than Lady Marry, whose hopes of a long, platonic association with her second cousin had been dashed with the flick of a shoe. Now she had to settle for a physically able man that she hated, or end up swinging from a scaffold.

"If I married Dratyew, I couldn't help myself," she said to Wanna. "I'd hold out for a year, maybe two—then one of us would slip. We could do it in our sleep. That happens, you know."

"Perhaps you could wear some sort of protective gear," Wanna said, thinking of Mr. Baits.

"Impossible," Lady Marry said. "I don't even like pyjamas."

●　●　●

Sir Dick saw his fiancée's torment. As a result, one evening he stopped Wanna in the corridor and asked her to step into the 34th Auxiliary Bedroom. "Wanna, is it?"

"Yes."

"I have a proposition for you." Sir Dick dragged a heavy Gladstone bag from under the bed. "Don't offer to help," he grunted snidely, the sinews sticking out on his arms. He hefted the bag onto the bed and extracted the contraption inside. It was a sharp-edged thing made of brass and iron, with tubes and wires and such sticking out every which way. There were two leather shoulder straps.

"Stand well back," he said, and gave the handle at the side a sharp tug. The machine sputted and futted, coughing out thick black smoke, then racketed to life.

"What is it?" Wanna yelled, over the insistent *pocketa-ta-pocketa*.

"Tracking device," Sir Dick said. "War surplus. I bought it off the Army. I'd like to you put it on Lady Marry."

"She'd never wear it! It must be twenty stone!"

"That's what the shoulder straps are for," Sir Dick said. "Tell her it's…a beauty treatment or something. Some female thing."

"I'm sorry, that's daft."

"I'll pay you."

"I won't do it." Wanna turned to leave.

"There's only a minor risk of explosion!"

"No, thank you."

Sir Dick prepared a choice word—but then a stray spark ignited the bed. By the time he doused it, Wanna was gone.

• • •

"Seems like old times," Miss O'Lyin said, as she and Dhumbas hunkered down in the courtyard. "Me and a fag. And a cigarette."

"Watch it."

"Well, forgive me, Mr. High-and-Mighty…" Miss O'Lyin took an angry drag. "Thinks he's the only one that can reappropriate words."

"I'd watch my tongue if I were you," Dhumbas said. "I'm going to be rich. I've bought a battleship from the Germans."

"You never."

"I have. It's called the *SMS München*."

"Where did you get the money for it?"

"Bought it on credit." Dhumbas exhaled blue smoke. "It's not just a battleship, it's also full of provisions—sugar, flour, cheese. Which I can sell to Mrs. Phatore, pay off the ship, and have a tidy little nest egg besides."

"Where will you sail it?"

"Where won't I? I might even shell the Abbey, who'll stop me?"

"The crazy police, that's who."

"Since when are you so enamored with Lord and Lady Knothead?"

"Never you mind. But I won't allow anyone to shell her ladyship."

"You'll change your tune when you see it," Dhumbas said, "everybody will. They'll say, 'There goes Dhumbas. I've heard he's got a 12-inch gun…Four, in fact."

The SMS München, in happier days. Dhumbas acquired the vessel from a gentleman he met at "Invert Mondays" at The Slap and Tickle. As usual, his scheme did not work out.

"Then rent yourself out at the circus. I'll believe it when I see it."

"Suit yourself."

● ● ●

For a while, Dhumbas' plan seemed to come off perfectly. He delivered some baking goods to the cook, and moored the *München* in Downturn's small pond, waiting to transfer the ship's massive stores to Mrs. Phatore.

That night, Mr. Cussin happened to look out of the windows of the library. "I say, m'lord—is that a German battleship in the pond?"

His lordship didn't even look up. "Don't be alarmed. I expect it's the Fairy Navy. Does it look like a pumpkin pulled by mice?"

There was a loud bang.

"What was that? Is Baits at it again?"

"We seem to have lost that plot-point." Mumbling how parodies used to have standards, the butler turned to me. "Percy, go downstairs and investigate."

When I got to the kitchen, Mrs. Phatore and Craisy were sitting on the floor, wreathed in smoke and stunned as a couple of haddocks. They were covered in scorchmarks and batter.

"Knew I shouldn't've trusted Dhumbas," the cook said as I helped her up. "That flour of his must've had gunpowder in it."

Craisy's eyes lit up in a frightening, feral way that I'd never seen before. "BRILLIANT!"

● ● ●

Dhumbas was sitting on the deck of his ship, dozing, dreaming of a life of wealth. Craisy and I crept by him, and down into the bowels of the vessel.

"Where is it all? I've never been on a ship before."

"How should I know?" I said. "Why did I let you talk me into this?"

"Someone had to row," Craisy said. "I'm just a wee lass."

"You're just a wee psycho."

"Don't be like that, Percy. I'll give you a kiss."

"Your kisses taste like kerosene."

Craisy ran ahead. We passed the Officer's Dayroom, where an empty couch beckoned. "You go on, wake me when you want to leave."

"But Percy, I've found it! Ooh! It's so much! It's like a dream!"

"Great," I said, "knock yourself out."

● ● ●

If every German battleship sank as quickly as the *München*, I can certainly see why the Huns lost the War. Mere moments after I'd placed my head on the red leather divan, there was a terrific explosion—and soon after that, the ship was at the bottom of the pond. I spotted Dhumbas in the midst of the wreckage. He looked angry enough to bite through iron, so I swam in the other direction.

Presently, Craisy paddled through the oil-streaked water.

"Craisy!" I yelled at the sooty, tattered figure. "What in blazes did you do?"

She wouldn't tell me. All she did babble, over and over, was "BLOODY BRILLIANT!"

CHAPTER THIRTEEN.

Moon, Swoon, Spoon
(1918 - April 1919)

Then—suddenly, savagely—came the Spanish Fly. Though little spoken of now, this was not an insect at all, but a microbe of the most devilish sort, whose main effect was to kindle irrational affections in the breast of those so afflicted. Mysterious, capricious, unpredictable, the Spanish Fly reshaped the world and left millions incredibly embarrassed in its wake. Such occurrences are common in the aftermath of war, and those prone to a more sentimental view of history suggest that this is a natural mechanism for the species to replenish itself. All I know is that 20 to 30 million people worldwide were created via the Spanish Fly, and most of them turned out to be a bad idea. They always seem to be in front of me at the Ripping P.O.

I can think of no place in England, and perhaps the world, less in need of the

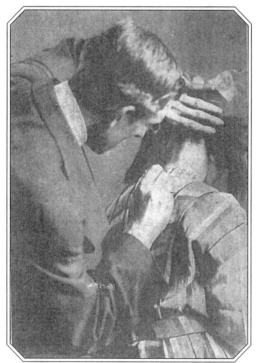

Spanish Fly than Downturn. The place was practically seething with romance, which was always the cause of the most vexatious troubles. First, of course, there was Wanna and her Mr. Baits, currently rotting in the stripy hole. Then Lady Marry, whose affections were quite possibly lethal. Mrs. Snughes' ex-boyfriend started World War I...and so forth.

In retrospect it is clear that the S.F. had been smoldering at Downturn Abbey for months before it emerged in earnest. How else to explain his

"If found, please return to..."
In the wake of the Fly, the Earl hired a
man to tattoo Downturn's address
on his daughters.

lordship's infatuation with a housemaid, Lady Edict's affection for a disembodied head, and Lady Unsybil's sudden decision that, of all the world's possibilities, the scraggle-faced Manson was the horse she'd bet on. And we mustn't forget Miss O'Lyin's laughable attachment to Dhumbas, Mr. Cussin's wet-eyed view of Lady Marry, Mrs. Phatore's relentless pursuit-by-proxy of Killem…Upstairs or downstairs, celibacy never looked so good. I can say without any fear of contradiction that love was the single worst thing ever to hit Downturn; without it the place might've been sane. All right, probably not, but a thing-boy can dream, can't he?

• • •

The explosion of the *SMS München*, though spectacular, did not arouse much comment inside Downturn. His lordship dismissed it as "faery fire," and that, apparently, was good enough. Certainly the house had other things on its mind: in a plot development we could all see at least three Chapters ago, Lady Unsybil had finally succumbed to the dark charms of Manson, the Gaelic chauffeur/Svengali.

"It's a youthful whim," her mother pleaded. "Or the Spanish Fly! You're not thinking clearly!"

"I don't care what you say, Mama." Lady Unsybil stood before a flabbergasted clan. "Charlie and I are going away to Ireland to start a commune."

"Of drug-addled thrill-killers, no doubt." The Earl's words dripped with scorn.

"If it comes to that!" Manson shot back. "Didn't the war teach you anything, man? This is a decadent culture, determined to consume everything it can grab— then dine on its own golden excrement until it finally collapses."

"Yeah!" Lady Unsybil said. "And *that's* why we've carved £s on our foreheads!"

"Prediction: bangs in three months," Lady Marry said.

Lady Edict was no more supportive. "This is what happens when you let a child nurse until seven."

"Thanks, Lady See-You-Next-Teatime! You too, Marry!"

"I cannot believe what is more galling," the Earl fumed, "that my youngest daughter is apparently determined to become some sort of industrial-strength Bohemian, or that my other daughters knew and didn't tell me."

"Don't blame me," Lady Marry said. "I saw an opportunity not to be the biggest slut in the family, and I seized it. Say what you like about Mr. Galoot, at least he wasn't Irish."

"Shh," Lady Violent said. "The American audience might hear you."

"I may be Irish, man," Manson said, " but you are all a bunch of squares."

His lordship wore a puzzled expression. "Marry, what did you mean just now? That bit about 'slut' and 'Mr. Galoot'?"

Her ladyship leapt into the breach. "So we're squares, Manson? And yet you've been perfectly content to take money from us for nearly a decade now."

"Just 'sticking it to The Man,' man."

Lady Violent was confused. "Who is this 'Man' you keep referring to?"

"It surely cannot be me," said the Earl, "I've shown you nothing but respect."

"Figure of speech, Papa." Lady Unsybil seemed to get more tangle-haired and vacant as the conversation went on.

"Yeah, man. The Man is the System."

"What System?" Lady Marry asked.

"That's also a figure of speech," Unsybil said. "Don't pretend like this is a surprise. Charlie and I have been leaving Statements of Rebellion around the house for weeks now."

Lady Cantswim gaped. "So it's *you* who's been leaving outrages in the potted palms? I assumed it was Lady Violent protesting Socialism."

"Would it help?" the old lady asked.

· · ·

I knew just how the Dowager Countess felt. Things were changing so quickly that any scrap of the good old days felt reassuring, even Dhumbas and Miss O'Lyin's conniving.

"When old Cussin stumbled out of the drawing room after Lady Unsybil dropped the bomb, his face was positively purple. I thought he was going to keel over right then and there."

"Leave it to him to spoil our fun," Miss O'Lyin said. For years, the pair had been betting to see which of them could trigger Mr. Cussin's inevitable heart attack. The kitty was up to £650.

"I really thought the Victrola would do it." Dhumbas had arranged so that Downturn's butler caught him in carnal relations with the device. Mr. Cussin had staggered, spluttered...and survived. Now, with the house on skeleton staff thanks to the 'Fly, our villains knew it was time to press their advantage.

"I think he's ready to crack," Miss O'Lyin said. "If only we could up the pressure, somehow. Maybe I'll do something nasty to Mr. Baits."

· · ·

At Downturn, the usual rum-ta-dum of pottiness seemed to be reaching fever-pitch. I tried to be an island of cool rationalism and forward-thinking; I even left copies of *Lo!* laying about the house whenever I'd finished reading them. But often that simply caused trouble, as when Mrs. Snughes called me into her sitting-room one evening.

"How's the narcolepsy?" I said.

"Never mind you and your tongue-twisters," she said. "Do you know because of you, Ethyl's gone mad?"

"Mrs. Snughes, I think Ethyl's always been a few colonies short of an Empire, if you don't mind my saying."

"Well, she's read that magazine of yours, and now she says she wants to freeze herself and the baby. Says she wants to stay frozen 'until mores change and unwed motherhood bears less of a social stigma.' As if that'll ever happen!"

"You might be surprised. Social reformer and scientist Marie Stopes said in the last issue that widespread birth control—"

"Again with that mouth! Do you know that Ethyl wants to be hung up in the ice house! Where will I put the hams? And her ladyship's furs?... Never mind, I just wanted you to know the trouble you've caused, in case you're keeping a running total." Mrs. Snughes got up. "Now come upstairs, you're needed in the dining room."

Me? A lowly thing-boy, waiting at table? This could be the break I'd been looking for!

"And don't get uppity—it's only temporary. Everyone's been affected by the Spanish Fly."

• • •

Mrs. Snughes was not kidding. When I shuffled into the dining room, smock filled with condiments, extra utensils, and a page of Arch One-Liners, just in case Lady Violent ran out, I saw the entire family in a state of semi-consciousness. The only footman was Mr. Marley, on loan from Mrs. Crawly, and he was standing in the corner laughing at nothing.

Wanna took Mrs. Snughes aside. "Mr. Marley was handling the cellar tonight because Mr. Cussin is ill. I think he served everyone malt liquor."

"Sorry," the fill-in footman said. "I ate one of Dad's medicinal scones by mistake. I'm higher than the Mongolfier Brothers."

Mrs. Snughes bristled. "Mr. Marley, I'll thank you to leave that kind of talk for the Herb Show and go downstairs immediately." She surveyed the damage. "Doesn't look like drunkenness to me, not the way her ladyship is making eyes at that soup tureen."

Indeed Lady Cantswim was cradling it, positively googly-eyed. "Oh, my darling…Oh, my dear little bowl…" she crooned.

"Cola, are you quite all right?" Lady Violent asked.

"Take her upstairs immediately, she's not at all well," his lordship said.

"I…I think I shall go, too," Lineolia declared. "I feel myself becoming quite attached to this napkin."

Sir Dick was so mean, he'd shoot at the weather.

"Leave it here," Lady Violent said. "Fear not, the heart is a resilient organ."

After her mother and Lineolia had departed, Lady Marry looked about the table. "My word, at this rate there'll be no one left."

"Except for me," Sir Dick declared. "I seem strangely bereft of all human feeling."

"Save anger and revenge. Don't forget about those."

"I never do," Sir Dick said. "My feeling is, if you love something, crush its spirit and destroy its soul."

Lady Marry imagined her future. "Whatever Marley poured, I need more of it."

•　•　•

The 'Fly killed in a very strange way. As you know, it caused an infatuation. Then, as the disease receded and the sufferer realized all the many things that stood between them and their love, the patient could die of a broken heart. When someone found themselves attracted to an inanimate object, as in the case of her ladyship, the condition was quite often lethal.

I stood next to Miss O'Lyin, handing over damp washcloths as she soothed the wheezing, retching, oozing noblewoman. Miss O'Lyin kept up a running monologue—Dr. Clarkson had said that it was important to keep the patient's spirits up at all costs.

"Of course it's possible for you to divorce your husband and marry the tureen," she said, swabbing vigorously. "The Spanish do that kind of thing all the time. And the Italians, too, I think."

"But...what will people say?"

"They'll be delighted, m'lady. Everyone likes soup. You won't be able to keep up with all the invitations."

"What about...Robber?"

"Oh, his lordship'll find someone new. Perhaps he'll meet a nice ladle. Then the four of you can double-date. That's what *I* think will happen."

"Thank you, O'Lyin, you always tell me the truth," Lady Cantswim murmured. I laughed out loud.

"Watch it," Miss O'Lyin said sharply, then turned to her slime-coated mistress, who had lapsed back into coma.

"The thing is, m'lady, I haven't. Not always." The guilt-wracked lady's maid pulled out a small leather book. On the front in gold script was embossed "My Misdeeds."

Miss O'Lyin cleared her throat and began. "In May 1906, I micturated into your soup. Knowing Cook, it probably improved it, but it was meanly meant and I regret it. Doesn't say here why I did it, but I'm sure I was quite cross with you, and if you'll forgive me for saying so, you probably deserved it. Later that summer..."

The litany went on for hours and hours. "...and that's how you lost your sense of smell. Dhumbas helped with some of it, m'lady, but he's weak in the mind. It was me, always me." Tears flowing, voice breaking, Miss O'Lyin claimed responsibility for everything from aphids in the garden to the assassination of French Socialist Jean Jaurès.

I could no longer contain myself. "Jaurès? That's preposterous."

"Who asked you? It was my day off, and he was acting uppity. "

"*Right.* And Dhumbas isn't gay, he's just saving himself for you."

Now I'd done it; Miss O'Lyin's eyes flashed fire. "You take that back, you little wretch! This was my tearful confession, my BAFTA moment, and now you've ruined it!"

I started to give her one back, but Miss O'Lyin's expression made me think better of it. I moved towards the door.

"That's right, get out of here, and bring me more washcloths. These are even snottier than you are."

I grabbed the cloths and left. But not before hearing, "Now, m'lady, about the Triangle Shirtwaist Fire..."

• • •

Some said that being in love already when the 'Fly hit conferred some protection; I'm no medico, but that was certainly borne out at Downturn. Wanna pointed this out to me that evening, when we were doing another load of snot-cloths.

"Thank God for Mr. Baits. I would've certainly snuffed it otherwise."

"How do you mean?"

"Think about it: Mr. Cussin got sick precisely when he and Lady Marry were on the outs. The Earl and her ladyship have been fighting for several episodes."

"Poor Lineolia," I said.

"But we knew she was doomed, just like Killem. So good and kind. Still, she and Mr. Crawly are a couple."

"Erm…"

"What did you see, Percy? Tell me."

"Well, when I was bringing this load of snot-cloths downstairs, I happened to walk by the Great Hall. Lady Marry and Mr. Crawly were playing the Victrola and—" I told what I saw.

"Oh, cousins do that kind of thing," Wanna said. "You'd know, if you grew up on a farm."

"But Wanna—Lineolia saw them."

"Really?" Wanna put down the cloth and wiped her hands. "I don't know about you, but if there's going to be a beat-down, I want to be there to hear it."

Five minutes later, we were kneeling at Lineolia's door. "I call the keyhole," Wanna said. That left me to lay on the floor and see what I could through the crack between the door and the carpet.

Lineolia lay on the bed, speaking weakly, glistening with sweat. Not for the first time that evening, I longed for an illness that made people look *better*.

"I saw you and Marry…Down in the Great Hall."

"Oh…crikey…That? It was nothing!" Mr. Crawly lied. "It's an old custom—a folk dance—"

"Please, Dratyew, don't lie. I'm from London…I know what that was."

"But Lineolia, why do you think morris-dancing is so popular? Not because it's cool, that's for bloody sure."

"I'm telling you, it doesn't bother me," Lineolia said. "In fact, when I saw it—when I saw you and Marry, I thought, 'Wow, she's done this before. I wonder how she keeps from gagging.'"

"Lineolia, we'll have our whole lives to practice. I don't mind."

"I…bet not," Lineolia wheezed.

"What I am trying to say is that there is nothing between Cousin Marry and

I—it was whatever Marley served at dinner—the stress of the wedding—"

"Dratyew, I'm dumping you."

"What?"

Lineolia pulled a sweaty, crumpled napkin from under the bedclothes.

"My dear! You were supposed to leave that downstairs!"

"True love knows no obstacles," Lineolia gasped. "His name is…Geoff. We're getting married. Please wish us well…as I wish for you and Marry."

•　•　•

At those words, Wanna took off like a flash—and I knew exactly where she was going: Mr. Baits' room.

Now, usually the sexes were segregated in the servants' quarters; but Mr. Baits' melancholy magnetism had moved the rules to be selectively broken, so that the locks were not. And once Mr. Baits' curious affliction became common knowledge, most of Downturn's female staff moved on, allowing Wanna and him to form a more durable, if thwarted, attachment.

Mr. Baits answered Wanna's knock with the muzzy look of someone freshly awoken. "Wuz wron'?"

Wanna grabbed him by the hand. "We're getting married!"

"What? Right now?"

"Yes," Wanna insisted. "Don't say no, I won't hear of it. It's a matter of life and death. Everyone here with shaky relationships is getting sick and dying."

"What about Lady Marry and Sir Dick?"

"That's not a relationship, that's a plot device to make viewers tear their hair out."

I mumbled something about glass houses and stones, and Wanna stuck her tongue out at me. "Percy knows of a way we can do it right now. He read it in one of his magazines, didn't you Percy?"

"Yes."

"And it's legal?"

"Totally legal," Wanna said.

"I don't know," Mr. Baits said. "I wouldn't want to involve you in my troubles—"

Wanna sneezed, on purpose. "Uh-oh. We'd better do it."

"But Wanna—"

"I do feel a headache coming on."

"My first marriage didn't turn out so well. Perhaps we could live together?"

"Percy, is it cold in here? Or is it just me, having the chills? And have you ever noticed how handsome your suspenders are?"

"All right, all right," Mr. Baits capitulated. "Let me get my robe."

• • •

"I do," Mr. Baits said into the receiver. "I'm sorry?…I said: 'I DO!'…No, 'do'! As in, 'Yes!'" He turned to me. "Bloody technology, only 1919 and already a crap idea."

"Stop complaining and hold it between us, so I can hear it!" Wanna said.

The upsurge in lightning matrimony caused by the 'Fly had led to a new invention: a phone service where, for a shilling a minute, couples could be connected to a live clergyman. This man of the cloth, on duty twenty-four hours a day, would perform the service via phone, resulting in a union recognized throughout the Commonwealth.

"You may not kiss the bride," a tinny voice said.

Mr. Baits blanched. "It's happening again. First the belt, now—"

I shouted, "I'm sorry, Reverend, could you say that louder?"

This time it was clear, much to everyone's relief. "You may now kiss the bride!"

As Mr. Baits and Wanna kissed, Mendelssohn's Wedding March played over the tiny tube. "You'll receive your license by Royal Mail. In that envelope will be a bill for one pound, ten and six. Please return your payment promptly, and may you have many years of happiness."

"Thank you," I said. Mr. Baits and Wanna had practically thrown down the

"If you agree to the terms of this marriage, say 'I do…' Now, hand the receiver to your wife…"

receiver so that they could make out. "When does the meter stop?"

"Who am I speaking with? The best man?"

"Yes. And the maid of honor, the ushers, the ringbearer, the whole lot."

"All right, the meter should be off now…Wish the happy couple well for me. And please, if they liked the service, could you ask them to tick that box on the short survey? My name is Reverend Mickleworth."

"Right. Thanks." The couple was stripping, which reminded me of something. "Wait, Reverend—before you go, do you happen to know how to get off a chastity belt?"

"Certainly. What model is it?"

"What model is it, Mr. Baits?"

"*Lacrima Aeterna 9000*," Baits gasped, the words garbled by Wanna's lips, face, *et cetera*.

I listened intently. "He says there's a little 'suicide switch' just along the taint."

"Taint? Where is that?"

"The midlands," I said. "'taint one end, and 'taint the other."

"Oh. What's it supposed to feel like?"

I passed the question to Reverend Mickleworth. "Feels like a little 'L', a slight protrusion," he said. "Just pull it towards the front, and—"

"Hurry Percy!" Wanna said.

"Mr. Baits! It's a little 'L'! Pull it towards your...'gentleman's obelisk'!"

"IT WORKED!" Mr. Baits roared. "Thank bloody Christ, it worked!"

"Get out of here, Percy!" Wanna said. "RUN!"

I didn't have to be told twice.

Mrs. Snughes told me they had to put potpourri in Mr. Cussin's office for a week.

●   ●   ●

Everyone was very happy for Mr. Baits and Wanna. Even Mr. Cussin talked brightly of "being finished with the smoldering glances and getting some real work done," and that was about as ebullient as he ever got. Certainly there was a change in Mr. Baits; even tasks he hated, like measuring all the gravel, were attacked with a whistle and a smile. It was love, surely—and bidding adieu to the *Lacrima Aeterna 9000*.

But even in life we are in death, so says the Bible, and especially at a place like Downturn Abbey. Happiness downstairs was balanced by sadness above, as dear, sweet, kind Lineolia kicked it, as we all knew she would. It was very sad to see her jilted fiancé drop a freshly laundered napkin into the grave. I caught Wanna's eye; among the throng, only she and I knew what it meant.

After the funeral, I saw Mr. Crawly and Lady Marry lingering, so I held back myself—just within earshot. After what Wanna and I had overheard through Lineolia's door, I wanted a sense of completion.

"Don't you see, Marry? We're cursed!" Mr. Crawly's voice was full of pain. Also, he was being filmed with a blue filter, which makes everything look miserable.

"I understand you're upset, and I share your feeling," Lady Marry said, "but 'cursed' seems to overstate it a bit."

"NO!" Mr. Crawly stepped outside of Lady Marry's umbrella, just to get rained on. "We are cursed, you and I, and it's better if we face up to it. We're both rich and beautiful, neither of us died in either the War or from the Spanish Fly, I was paralyzed, but made a miraculous recovery, and you have managed to alienate a series of suitors, but the heir to Downturn still thinks you're hot as Flanders in July!" Mr. Crawly glared upwards at the leaden, weeping sky. "CURSED! CURSED! CURSED!...We shall never be happy!"

"Well, you might have something with that last bit..."

•   •   •

Others at Downturn had better reason to complain, as I found out when I arrived back downstairs. The whole corridor was filled with policemen, and Mrs. Snughes grabbed my ear.

"Percy, I told you that telephone marriage was never legal!" she said, giving it a savage twist.

"Let him go, Mrs. Snughes," Mr. Baits said, resigned. "It's not about that. It's about my wife."

"No it's not, sir," the policeman interjected. "I mean, it might be, sometime in the future. But currently, the charge is—what's the phrase, Sergeant?"

"Wilfull torturin' of the audience."

"But that's impossible!" Wanna said.

"I'd stay quiet, Miss. From what I hear, you might well be an accessory." The cop turned to Mr. Baits. "Over and over again, if you'd merely said something— told the truth, or defended yourself, like a normal person—"

"I don't deny it."

"See, there! You're doing it again!"

"It's all right!" Mr. Baits said. "Don't worry about me! Even if I have to rot in prison, I'll never—"

"Take him away, Sergeant. Take him away."

CHAPTER FOURTEEN.

Goodbye to All That Crap
(Christmas 1919-1920)

It was difficult to have much Christmas spirit that year, knowing that as we celebrated at Downturn, Mr. Baits was likely being forced to play valet to "Big Clive." Still, we all slapped on brave faces and tried to make the best of it, in the English way. A tree was trimmed. Crackers were pulled. Gifts were exchanged.

"Thank you, m'lady," Wanna said, holding up a file.

"It's traditional," Lady Marry said lightly. "Percy, what do you think of your present? I picked it out myself."

I looked at the scrap of weathered parchment, covered with blotchy runes and diagrams. "It's…very nice, m'lady. What is it?"

"A map to the Downturn Hoard," Lady Violent interjected, en route to a potty break. "People have been looking for that since my grandfather was a girl."

After the Dowager Countess trundled out of earshot, Lady Cantswim glided over. "I think Cousin Violent's losing it a little," she murmured.

"May be, Mama, but you needn't be so gleeful." Lady Marry turned back to me. "Our clan buried a bunch of things, to keep them away from Cromwell. All of it should be terrifically valuable by now. Do you think you're up to the task?"

"Probably not," I said.

Sir Dick loudly criticized my "can't do" spirit, but Lady Marry laughed. "Give thing-boy credit, at least he's honest. I believe in you, Percy, old chap. Don't forget the rest of us when you're loaded."

"Loaded" was the proper term, all right…but I'm getting ahead of my story.

•   •   •

Later that night, as I sat at the long servants' table puzzling over my map, Dhumbas and Miss O'Lyin were playing with their own present, a Quija board.

"'It…was…worth…it,'" Miss O'Lyin spelled out. "Sincerely…Galoot.'"

"Foreigners are so bloody romantic." Dhumbas looked at me. "Come over here, Percy. Let's let the board have a go at your map."

"No thanks." I got up and left; the last thing I wanted was for that thieving footman to swipe my treasure. I decided to hide the map in my underwear as I slept.

Out in the corridor, I passed Mrs. Hughes' office. She was talking to Wanna. "Did you see what Mrs. Crawly gave the Dowager Countess? A Dr. Osbert's

'Silver Sceptre.'"

Wanna spat medicinal scone. "She never!"

"With all fourteen attachments. If it had been anyone else, I might have thought there was a subtext. But clueless *and* medical? That's Isapill Crawly all over."

"Are all great families so dirty?"

"How do you think they keep going?" Mrs. Hughes asked. "The Dowager Countess had the last laugh. She said, 'At my age, the friction will probably set me ablaze.' Mr. Cussin turned the most delightful shade of mauve."

Wanna grew glum. "I'll be propositioning Dr. Osbert myself soon."

"Don't talk like that." Mrs. Snughes patted Wanna's hand. "Mr. Baits is innocent, and he'll be back before you know it."

•   •   •

I doubted that, somehow, especially after hearing what his lordship said to Mr. Crawly. We'd all gone down to York for the trial; my smock was stuffed so full of hankies, it was difficult to fit through doorways.

"I feel so powerless," Mr. Crawly complained. "This case is out of my area. I wish Baits had inhaled asbestos, or been maimed in a slag fire or something."

"We all do," Lady Marry said.

"Yes, don't blame yourself," agreed the Earl.

"That will be difficult. Did I tell you I'm cursed?"

"Please ignore my idiot child," Mrs. Crawly mumbled.

"You'll see, mother…Cousin Robber, who's representing Mr. Baits?"

"A gentleman by the name of Murky."

"Is he good?" Wanna asked.

"I think he's handled cases like this before," his lordship said, "if that counts for anything. Baits told me the chap was recommended by his old matrimonial agency. Apparently their clients go through this a lot."

Lady Marry pointed. "I think that's him now."

Short, moustachioed, and almost as well-padded as I was, Mr. Murky introduced himself. "Let us get down to business. We haven't much time."

"What is your defense?" Mr. Crawly asked.

"Well, Mr. Baits refuses to say that he didn't do it, so as not to injure the unknown person or persons who did."

Mrs. Crawly gasped. "That's insane."

The Earl nodded sadly. "Perhaps, but it's fairly standard operating procedure for my valet."

"As I have gathered," Murky said. "But without Mr. Baits actually denying anything, I've been forced to fall back to my next line of defense."

"Which is?" Mrs. Crawly asked.

"That his boss told him not to do anything foolish."

"Meaning, Papa? Generalissimo of the Fairy Forces?"

"Yes."

"He's done for, he's done for!" Wanna wailed.

"There there," his lordship said. "I'll put things right. You'll see."

•   •   •

And the Earl did put things right—right in the crapper.

It was a special kind of agony, watching him flail there in the dock. In his lordship's defense, his logical faculties were severely undernourished. He hadn't had to justify or explain, much less defend, any of his actions for decades. He was like some miraculous fish, perfectly suited to its deep-sea environment which, when hauled up to the surface, explodes, showering everyone with offal.

The prosecution was merciless. "'Because I said he didn't' is not an answer to the question. Nor is 'Does he *look* like a murderer?'."

"I object!" the Earl said.

"You can't object," the judge said. "Please answer the question."

"Erm…I've forgotten it."

Next to me in the gallery, Wanna facepalmed. The prosecutor repeated the question. "Did Mr. Baits say anything creepy in regards his late ex-wife?"

The Earl thought. Then he reached down and tied his shoe. Then, he extracted a medicinal scone and nibbled at it.

"Your lordship?"

"I'm thinking! I'm thinking!" The Earl dropped his scone. He leaned down, ostensibly to pick it up, but I think he was going to make a run for it. So did the judge.

"Leave it. The Court insists that the witness stop phumphering."

His lordship gave a truly miserable sigh. "Mr. Baits said, 'One day my wife will stuck her nose into the wrong thing.'"

There was an audible gasp; Mr. Baits was done for. Still, at least one life was saved that day—I just managed to grab Wanna before she could leap the railing and throttle her employer.

•   •   •

When Wanna and I went to see the doomed valet, he took it a lot better than she did. "Thank them all. Don't blame Mrs. Snughes and Miss O'Lyin. And thank his lordship. Tell him...tell him that, with a defense like that, who needs a prosecution?"

Wanna brushed away a tear. I said the only cheerful thing I could think of. "Look on the bright side, Mr. Baits: Everybody downstairs totally thinks you're a badass."

"I suppose that's something, Percy. Wanna, will you kiss me? One last time?"

Wanna looked at me. "Turn away, Percy. Give us some privacy."

I don't know exactly what happened next, but I know everyone learned a very important lesson: A file is much too big to hold in your mouth.

• • •

With such sad news, everyone at Downturn did their best to carry on. The only one who seemed truly unaffected was Dhumbas. Showing his unerring ability to read people and situations, the evil first footman walked into Mr. Cussin's office one morning doing a little soft-shoe, and whistling a happy tune.

Downturn's butler looked up from his ledger with a string of curses; as usual, the household accounts had told him one thing: standards were declining. "Yes, Dhumbas?"

"Now that Mr. Baits isn't coming back, I was wondering if I might have his old job?"

"Is this an actual request, Dhumbas," Mr. Cussin said, "or yet another of your and Miss O'Lyin's gambits to give me a heart attack? Yes, I've known for years. Life is its own reward, but I cannot pretend that spiting you both doesn't give me added pleasure."

"Oooh, burn," I said softly, not looking up from my map.

Dhumbas was completely unmanned. "I...don't know what to say, Mr. Cussin."

"Luckily, I do. I've spoken to his lordship, and he feels that you should take a long walk off the short portico bordering the pond."

Dhumbas' face fell. "I knew it. He doesn't trust me. Because of the stealing."

"No, he just hates people with brown hair! *Of course* it was the stealing!"

"But why keep me on, then?"

"I trust you lived through the middle of this season? If you weren't around, we'd all die of boredom."

• • •

My first thought when I heard that the Earl's dog had gone missing was that it was a euphemism for something; I'd lived at Downturn long enough to know what the family was like. But when it turned out to be literally the problem at hand, I was glad—not because I disliked Whatsit, but because I was hungry for diversion. I had officially declared myself defeated by my treasure map. Downturn's Hoard would have to wait for a more worthy intellect than mine. After weeks of torment, where its smudgy ciphers had swum before my eyes even during sleep, I was not merely resigned to give up trying, I was delighted to.

But Fate had something different in store for me.

Upstairs and down came together to search for the dog, scouring the dark woods for any signs of canine activity. I was tasked to circulate among the participants, distributing lamps, mecurochrome and chewing gum as needed. When I passed by Dhumbas, I could smell the liquor on his breath.

"Where is she? Why did I do it? *Why?*"

I immediately sussed out Dhumbas had attempted something stupid with the dog. "You know, you're just not cut out for this," I said, not altogether unkindly. "You give it your best, Lord knows. But none of your schemes ever come to fruition. It's actually quite excruciating to watch."

"I know! I know!" He pounded his head with his fists. "Just! Not! Smart! Enough!"

"What I can't understand is, where do you get the ideas then? Do you subscribe to some sort of newsletter or something? *Evil Footman Fortnightly?*"

Dhumbas wandered off without answering, still excoriating himself.

"I'd demand a refund!" I yelled after him.

I was getting cold, so I ambled back in the direction of the Abbey. Presently I stumbled upon Mr. Crawly and Lady Marry, who were engaged in a private chat. Wanting to respect their privacy, I did not announce myself, instead crouching in a small depression behind a shrub.

"But you don't know that I'd be grossed out to next Michaelmas. I might surprise you. I might be into it."

"You wouldn't be," Lady Marry said.

"Is it a tattoo?"

"Dratyew, really—"

"A piercing, then. That's not so unknown among our sort. They don't call them 'Prince Albert's for nothing, you know."

"All right, I'll tell you…"

I didn't pay attention to what Lady Marry said next—partly because I was there when it happened, back in Chapter Whatever-it-was, and partly because the depression I was huddled in seemed to be sliding a bit under my weight, as if it weren't solid. I put my hand down, to prevent myself from falling into the clearing where Lady Marry and Mr. Crawly were gabbing...and touched metal.

I dug at it, more out of surprise than anything, and presently had revealed the outlines of a torso-sized metal cask.

"I'm confused," Mr. Crawly said. "But how did you kill him?"

"I'd be the last to know," Lady Marry said sadly. "I was rather distracted. I was simply copying a pair of camels I once saw at the zoo."

"Excuse me," I said.

"One moment, Percy. Cousin Marry, have you tried it with other men? In the spirit of scientific discovery?"

"I'm afraid your intellectual curiosity is greater than mine," Lady Marry said.

"Yoo-hoo, knotheads! Something of note has occurred!"

Mr. Crawly mused, "Suddenly your marriage to Sir Dick makes a grim kind of sense."

"Indeed," Lady Marry replied. "If he tried any funny business, I'd rid the world of an enormous tit, and inherit a fortune in the bargain."

"EXCUSE ME!"

"Not now, Percy! Can't you see Lady Marry and I are explicating a plot-point?"

"But I've found it," I said. "I've found the Hoard!" I held up the lid-top, which had rusted free.

"So you have." Lady Marry was grateful for a less painful topic. "Cousin Dratyew, let's help him take it back to the house."

"We're not finished talking about this," Mr. Crawly said.

"I suspect we aren't."

•   •   •

The servants hall echoed with my outrage. "A bunch of makeup? That's all?"

"I'm afraid so," Mrs. Snughes said, sorting through the pile of rusted, earth-smelling items jumbled on the table. There were lipsticks, rouge, tins of face-powder. "Cromwell outlawed it all. I suppose the ladies of the house buried it. Then after they died, the legend grew. Trinkets became treasure."

Everyone was sorry for me, I could tell by the looks on their faces. Everyone, that is, except Dhumbas.

"I guess you're just not cut out for it, Percy old chap. You give it your best, Lord knows..." He picked up a large flagon of fluted rose-colored glass, pulled the cork, and sniffed it. "Cheer up, everyone—this smells alcoholic."

"Oh I wouldn't," Mrs. Phatore said with a grimace. "Probably poisonous by now."

"Let's ask the spirits," Craisy said, and roped Miss O'Lyin into the effort. Two minutes later, Craisy looked up, utterly flummoxed. "I don't understand. What's it mean?"

Miss O'Lyin stared at Dhumbas. "Woof woof. I'm locked in the bloody shed."

●　●　●

I passed the next day or two in a haze of disappointment and rage at Oliver Cromwell. "At least you found it, Percy old bean," his lordship said to me the next evening. "Nobody else can say that."

Before I could respond, there were loud voices and the sounds of a commotion. The Earl put down the fairy tuxedo he was knitting, and took off like a shot in the direction of the library, with me trailing close behind.

"What's going on here?" he shouted.

Mr. Crawly and Sir Dick were rolling around on the rug, grappling and swearing. Like the man of action he was, His lordship stripped off his jacket, strided over, and awarded Mr. Crawly the match.

"The winner!" he said, raising Mr. Crawly's arm aloft.

"Knew I wouldn't get a fair referee here," Sir Dick said, struggling to his feet. "It was fixed from the start." The media magnate smoothed his hair, and wiped the blood off his lip. Then he pointed at each of us and said, "Unfriend, unfriend, unfriend."

His lordship's dog simply wasn't the same after his night in the shed. He grew his hair long, and began treating himself for "the megraine."

"What's that mean?" the Earl asked.

"You'll find out someday," Sir Dick said, and stalked out.

• • •

The next morning—the one of Mr. Baits' execution—Mr. Cussin ran through the Great Hall with a telegram. "M'lord! This just arrived!"

The Earl fiercely ripped the envelope open. Out fell four coupons for Speedball Cola. (Lady Unsybil's change-of-address hadn't gone through.)

"Oh, and also this came." Mr. Cussin handed over another envelope. This time, the Earl's tearing was justified.

"Thank God!" he said. "Baits' sentence has been commuted."

"I knew they wouldn't hang him, not during a Christmas episode," her ladyship said.

I piped up. "Do they give a reason, m'lord?"

"Why, Percy?" Mr. Cussin growled. "Planning to be tried for murder?"

It was nice to see his lordship so relieved. "Relax, Cussin. There's no impertinence in the face of good news. They say it was the chastity belt. While it doesn't excuse the murder, the Minister believes it is an extenuating circumstance."

• • •

And so joy returned to Downturn Abbey. While Mr. Baits was not free, he would remain available to keep the plot bubbling for at least another season. Dhumbas and Miss O'Lyin, the two worst employees in the history of service, would be kept on, as well. Sir Dick would almost certainly be on the warpath, and personally, if you ask me, we probably haven't seen the last of Captain Head, either.

Everyone was on their best behavior at the Servants' Ball— except for Dhumbas, of course; he had stolen the flagon of 300-year old perfume from my dresser, and spiked the punch with it. It is unclear to me whom he was planning to poison, but if I'd been taught anything from my time at Downturn, it was that Dhumbas' plots never bore up well under scrutiny. And as it happened, the

Dhumas "pre-gamed" for the Servants' Ball by huffing mothballs.

elixir wasn't poisonous in the least—but it did pack quite a wallop. So much so that after three sips, Lady Edict came over all egalitarian-like.

"Percy, go to the North Gallery, and invite all the men there to come to the servants' dining area for a cup of this delightful punch."

"The men? The ones holding up the building?"

"Quite. The ex-orphans."

"I don't think you're ever an *ex*-orphan, m'lady, but I catch your meaning… Won't the building collapse?"

"Don't be a spoilsport, Percy. It's the Twenties now. What did your magazine call it? 'A time of carefree hedonism were the grim realities of life were shucked away'? Stop arguing and start shucking."

•   •   •

The liquored-up ex-orphans refused to stay downstairs and, emboldened by Lady Edict's punch, demanded that I escort them to the dancefloor. I considered declining, but holding up a building is rough work, and taking on all those steel-muscled alumni of the Foundling Home was well above my abilities. However, I decided to make myself scarce, in case something happened and blame needed assigning.

I was shutting a window on the second floor, and preparing to mount the stairs to the servants' quarters and a warm bed, when I overheard Lady Marry and Mr. Crawly. Standing outside in the cold, they were, as usual, engaged in a deeply personal conversation, and I protected them from embarrassment by not telling them I could hear every word.

"Quite an evening," Mr. Crawly said.

"Feel free to thank me," Lady Marry replied. "I was the one who slipped £5 to the band to play the Lambada."

"I could've gone my entire life without seeing Cussin jitterbug," Mr. Crawly said. "Is the chest-clutching part of it, or is that Cussin's own interpretation?

Lady Marry laughed. "That's a sight I will remember in America."

"So you're going."

"Perhaps I'll go out to Hollywood, and get involved in some titanic scandal. I seem to have a talent for it."

"I can see it now," Mr. Crawly said, miming a headline. "'Aristo-Vamp Nabbed in H'wood Love Nest with Goat, Chaplin, Mentholatum.'"

The pair stood in silence, and naturally I was quiet, too. Suddenly, the night was rent by the most amazing crash, as Downturn's unsupported North Gallery gave way. Ragged cheers issued from the vicinity of the dance floor.

"What in blazes was that?"

"Your ideal of me, I expect," Lady Marry said. "Or it could be a metaphor."

"For what? I'm too drunk."

"End of an era, changing times," Lady Marry replied. "Oh, who gives a damn? We'll clean it up in the morning."

"I'm still having trouble wrapping my head around this," Mr. Crawly said. "First guy out of the box—"

"Into it."

"—the very first one," Mr. Crawly said, "and he just…died."

"That's about the size of it."

"Marry, forgive me for saying this, but you must be some amazing lay."

She was shocked. "You don't despise me?"

"Are you kidding? I could no more despise you than despise that roller coaster at the Ripping Village Fair, the one that's breaking all the time and occasionally kills people."

Lady Marry's shoulders sagged. "How come that doesn't make me feel any better?"

"But it should, Marry." Mr. Crawly took her hands in his. "You see, whenever a roller coaster kills someone, there are two types of men: those who want it torn down immediately, and those who queue up to ride it. Guess which type I am?"

Lady Marry's eyes were shining. "Oh, Dratyew, is it true? You'd risk your life like that for me?"

"Once a day, and twice on Sunday. More, when oysters are in season."

"Oh, Dratyew! But you might die."

"Perhaps, my love—but what a way to go."

THE END
(For now.)

ABOUT THE AUTHOR.

....

Michael Gerber has delighted (and perhaps infuriated) millions with his parodies, humorous novels, and YA fiction. His first book, *Barry Trotter and the Shameless Parody*, became a worldwide sensation, selling 850,000 copies and reaching #2 on *The London Times* bestseller list. His work has been translated into 25 languages, and seems to be especially funny in Polish, for some reason.

Before writing novels, Mr. Gerber contributed humor to *The New Yorker*, *The New York Times*, "Saturday Night Live," and many other venues, great and small. He lives in Santa Monica, California, with his wife and one very loud cat.

He can be reached via his website, www.mikegerber.com, and on Facebook.

AUGUST 1917 · *Vol. XXI, No. 8*

LO!

A Journal of What Will Be

"In fifty years, all popular music will be amplified. At the end of the performance, this musician will purposely destroy his apparatus onstage, to provide a nihilistic crescendo."—*Prof. R.N. Van Buskirk (Oxon.)*

PRICE: 6d

(buy now—much higher in future)

ACKNOWLEDGMENTS.

Every project chooses its own path to completion, and as *Downturn Abbey*'s route was particularly rock-strewn and circuitous, I am especially grateful to everyone who helped along the way. This book would not have made it to publication without the infinite patience, love, and frankly terrifying competence of my wife, Kate Powers; anyone who laughs at *Downturn* (even a little) owes her a Starbucks drink of her choice. I personally would not have made it to publication, were it not for the love and generosity of my parents, Greg and Patricia Gerber, who have encouraged me and laughed at my jokes since before the beginning. To all the dear friends and relations, dedicated doctors, and well-wishers foreign and domestic: thank you. No person could be luckier than I. I hope you enjoyed *Downturn Abbey*.

JOLLY GOOD EGGS.

Downturn Abbey was funded via Kickstarter.com, a crowdfunding site where readers can pledge money to help worthy projects happen. Though all the book's backers have my deep thanks, the following donors were particularly instrumental:

Susan Brady	Josh Gilbert
Tom Powers	Ilya Kushnirsky
Matthew Fogel	Larry J. Powers
Trish Gerber	Maureen Powers
Don Watson	Jonathan Schwarz
Karen Backus	Linda Logan
Rupa Shah	Barry Burland

...and the three eminent worthies who put us over the top,
Jerry Neufeld-Kaiser
Whitney Neufeld-Kaiser
Tho Dinh